To Miriam,

The Fisherman

with love

Mary Jane Forbes

Mary Jane Forbes

Todd Book Publications

The FISHERMAN

Copyright © 2013 by Mary Jane Forbes
All rights reserved. No part of this book may be used or reproduced by any means, graphic, electronic, or mechanical, including photocopying recording, taping or by any information storage retrieval system without the written permission of the publisher except in the case of brief quotations embodied in critical articles and reviews.

This is a work of fiction. All of the characters, names, locations, incidents, organizations, and dialogue in this novel are either the products of the author's imagination or are used fictitiously. The views expressed in this work are solely those of the author.

ISBN: 978-0-9847948-5-0 (sc)
Printed in the United States of America
Todd Book Publications: 7/2013
Port Orange, Florida

Author photo: Ami Ringeisen
Cover design: Mary Jane Forbes

To Marcia,

A most wonderful hostess!
I hold dear my memory of curling up on your swing, a gentle sway as I tapped my toe on the mosaic tiles, glass of wine in hand, gazing out the French doors to the blue waters of the Gulf.

Thank you!

Books by Mary Jane Forbes

FICTION

Murder by Design, Series:
Murder by Design – Book 1
Labeled in Seattle – Book 2
Choices, And the Courage to Risk – Book 3

Novel
The Baby Quilt … *a mystery!*
The Message…Call Me!

Elizabeth Stitchway, Private Investigator, Series:
The Mailbox – Book 1
Black Magic, An Arabian Stallion – Book 2
The Painter – Book 3
Twister – Book 4
The Fisherman – Book 5

House of Beads Mystery Series:
Murder in the House of Beads – Book 1
Intercept – Book 2
Checkmate – Book 3
Identity Theft – Book 4

Short Stories
Once Upon a Christmas Eve, a Romantic Fairy Tale
The Christmas Angel and the Magic Holiday Tree

NONFICTION
Authors, Self Publish With Style

Visit: www.MaryJaneForbes.com

Florida Locations

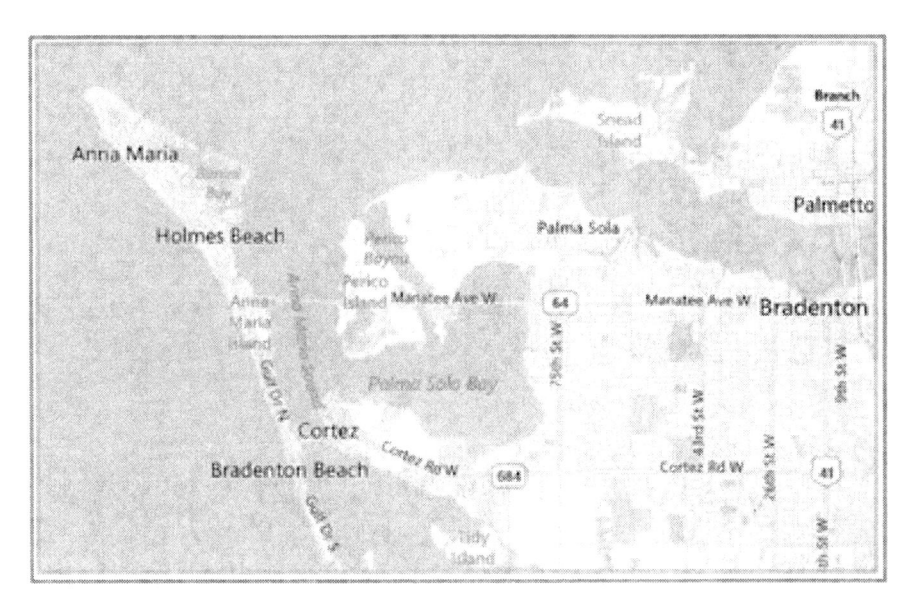

Characters

<u>The Parsons</u>
Dr. Charles & Doris Parsons
Patty Sue Parsons
Regina Parsons

<u>The Macintyres</u>
Daniel Macintyre
Charles Daniel Macintyre (Mac)
Crew: Sissy, Shrimp, Studs

<u>Friends</u>
Dr. Maria Grayson
Marianne Grayson
Madame Crystal, Psychic

Acknowledgements

Captain Kathe Fannon and First Mate Pup-Pup: Thank you for the inspirational tour of the waters around Cortez from the Star Fish Market dock, especially sliding off the bow of your tour boat into the warm Gulf waters looking for seashells and urchins.

Patti McKee, Sandbar Restaurant: You are the ultimate beach wedding planner. Your stories of some of the traditions that have developed from such special events were a highlight of my stay on Anna Maria Island.

Rick Catlin, The Islander Newspaper: Your *Ghost Bride* article started the juices flowing. Thank you for your initial guidance of points of interest on Anna Maria Island.

Captain Tim Garrett and his wife Lisa, WaterProof Sports Fishing Charter, Ponce Inlet: Thank you for giving me a glimpse into the charter fishing business. The afternoon frenzy when you docked: the welcoming back from family and friends that day, the picture taking of over four-hundred pounds of fish hanging on the sign, and then your passengers strutting proudly off to their cars with their cleaned, filleted, and ice-packed fish—fabulous.

Peggy Keeney: Thanks for your tenacious editing. Our discussions, over a mug of coffee or a glass of wine, made for a far better read. You are wonderful.

Captain Roger Grady and his wife Pat: Thank you for your words of encouragement, reviewing the manuscript, finding inconsistencies or something requiring more explanation, and setting me straight on all things boating. Thanks to your son-in-law, Mike Young, for his help wagering a boat in a poker game.

Gail Shepherd: Thank you for your expert perspective in bringing the hospital scenes to life.

Carol Ann Appio, Psychometry and Photo Analysis: Thank you for the reading! Your skill gave depth to the psychic character, Madame Crystal.

Molly Tredwell: Thank you for your help in moving the characters along on their emotional journey. I could never do this without your unwavering support.

The
Fisherman

Part One
Chapter 1

August First
Anna Maria Island, Florida

Patty Sue Parsons twirled in her bridal gown beaming with joy. In three days she would marry her prince, a strong, handsome fisherman with dark wavy hair, a stark contrast to her waist-length, silky blond curls. Her mother sitting on a straight chair, her sister and her best friend perched on the bed were enthralled watching the angel spin around the master bedroom.

She bent over her mother, kissing both rouged cheeks. "Mother, thank you for arranging this wonderful beach house. The last three weeks have been heavenly."

Doris Parsons jerked back in surprise at the rare display of affection between herself and her daughter.

Giggling, the bride darted from the bedroom and down the short hall to the great room—open spaces flowing from one to the next—a cozy living room outlined by a curved couch facing a television and coffee table overflowing with bridal magazines. The dining area's long table was separated from the couch by a swing anchored on shiny steel chains bolted to the ceiling. The swing, perfect for two, faced

French doors opened wide to a line of trees and the melody of Gulf waters lapping the white sandy beach.

The curvy couch and swing were puffed up with soft cushions in heavy cotton sprinkled with flowers in dusty blue, yellow, green, and pink. They beckoned anyone passing by to sit, curl up with a book or for an intimate conversation.

The bride swished out the French doors to the narrow deck, grasped the white railing throwing her head back to breathe in the moist summer air. Stepping back through the doors, she raised her hands to the ceiling twirling about, then playfully lowered her slim figure to the swing.

"For God's sake, stop. You're making me dizzy," her sister snipped flopping on a ladder-back chair beside the swing. Her only sibling, Regina was older by two years and, if truth be told, wished she was the sister in the long white gown.

"Oh, come on, sister dear, my maid-of-honor, I'll not let you cast a gloomy spell over the next three days. If I want to dance, smile, laugh and cry tears of joy, you'll not stop me." Patty Sue smiled at her sister who seemed mellow the first two weeks of their stay at the beach house accepting the fact that Danny had not chosen her, had turned sullen once again. And, Regina's mood seemed to be spreading because Patty Sue caught Marianne, her bridesmaid, wiping a tear away when she thought no one was looking.

Of course, Doris Parsons was always starched, her long pointy face turning particularly sour once she heard her precious baby had chosen a commercial fisherman for her husband.

Patty Sue ignored their dour faces.

"She's right, Regina. Button it." Mrs. Parsons snatched her purse lying on the dining room table. "Where is that seamstress? I thought you said Millie promised to be here on the dot of one o'clock. You can't trust anyone to keep their word these days. No consideration. I made lunch reservations."

Because of the tension that enveloped the family after announcing her engagement, Patty Sue decided there would be no parties—no bridal showers, no girl's final night on the town, and no rehearsal dinner. She was not going to look at long faces, and definitely would not put up with their nasty comments about her fisherman. The only celebration she accepted was the luncheon today.

"When's Father coming?" Patty Sue asked turning to her mother.

"Friday. I told him not to struggle up the stairs with the suitcases I packed for the remaining week of our stay. If I'm not here when he arrives be sure to show him the elevator to the second floor. I don't want him to pull his back out."

Regina shot a look at her mother. "He doesn't have a back problem … more something in his head from talking to all of his buddies at the men's club, lifting a scotch on the rocks while sucking on a Cuban cigar."

Doris gasped. "Regina, don't be nasty. Thanks to him you girls were presented at the debutante ball." Doris smoothed a nonexistent strand of blond hair back to her chignon held in place with pearl studded combs. "Your father deserves his time away from his patients, the lectures, and social events we're obligated to attend. It's not easy listening to their troubles, prescribing sedatives so they can carry on with their lives. Not easy at all."

Hearing a knock, Doris strode to the door. "Finally, that seamstress."

"Hi, Mrs. Parsons."

"Oh, you're not who I expected."

"Sorry, but you'll love what I have for you—a bouquet of flowers and some tea cookies. Your friend, I guess this is her house, ordered them for you." The young woman brushed by Doris to the large island separating the kitchen from the rest of the great room. Setting the vase of flowers and the box of cookies down on the black granite counter, she turned to look at Patty Sue. "Oh, my, your dress is beautiful."

"Thank you," Patty Sue said. Fishing around in her large tote on the chair at the end of the dining room table, she pulled out a Polaroid instamatic camera. "Would you mind taking a picture of us? Actually, snap it four times so we each have one," she giggled handing the camera to the girl.

The women huddled together on the swing, mother and daughter in the center, Regina and Marianne on either end.

"Nice. Say cheese," the girl said smiling pulling the picture as it spit out of the camera. "You want three more?"

"Yes, please," Patty Sue said grasping Marianne's hand and her mother's on the other side, Doris's eyebrows shot up at the touch.

The women continued to huddle, three strained faces pulling their lips to a tight smile and the joyful bride glowing in the center as the flash sparked three more times. Lining the pictures up on the dining room table, Patty Sue exclaimed they were perfect then handed them out as the delivery girl took one last look around, catching the dazzling bride in the sunbeams streaming through the windows as she left.

Tucking her copy of the Polaroid in her purse, Marianne strolled behind Patty Sue. "How are you going to wear your hair? Up in a twist or long over your shoulders?" she asked as the bride preened in front of the French doors imagining that Danny was watching, smiling at her from the sea.

"I don't know. What you do you think? A French twist would look very sophisticated topped with my jeweled crown holding the veil," Patty Sue replied twisting her curls behind her head.

"Personally, if I had your wavy golden hair I would let it flow down my back. With the crown you will be the picture of a fairy princess," Marianne said smiling at her best friend.

Doris checked her watch for the umpteenth time, sighed, raising her head to the ceiling. "Where is that woman? I want to show her where your gown should be nipped in at the waist, accentuate your figure."

"Mother, you three go on to the restaurant. Millie should be here any minute ... I'll catch up with you. Order me a champagne cocktail. I plan to enjoy these three days. Now, scoot."

"All right, but don't dawdle. I hung your sundress in the closet along with your other outfits and your going-away costume. Be sure Millie knows to really pinch in your waist. You have no stomach, so she shouldn't have any trouble."

Marianne kissed the porcelain cheeks of the beautiful bride as she left with the other two navigating the stairs to the ground floor, then out the garage and up the street to the corner to catch the trolley—a brightly painted little bus on wheels with white hubcaps, the lower half painted in the blue of the Gulf water and the top outlined with the orangey-yellow of the sunshine. Anna Maria Island provided the complimentary trolley ran the full seven-mile length of the island picking up and dropping off smiling passengers to shop, eat, and enjoy all the island had to offer.

Alone in the house, Patty Sue scampered out the French doors to the end of the deck peeking around the railing. Not seeing her seamstress she floated back to the swing, perched on the flowered cushion pushing a rhythmic sway with her toe, dreamily looking out at the Gulf's sapphire water twinkling back at her through the fluttering leaves of the trees. She imagined her groom at the helm of his boat bringing in his week's load of fish.

Everyone liked Daniel Macintyre, a hulk of a man five years older than her twenty-two. He pursued Patty Sue, courted her since the day they met on the pier in New Orleans. He had known her for several years as a scrawny teenager but hadn't taken notice until that day. She was working at the café next to the dock, a summer job before her senior year at Tulane. On her afternoon break, she stood on the dock watching him as he skillfully pulled into the slip with his heavy load of snapper, grouper, and mullet delivering thousands of pounds of fish. The day they met, as today, was also the first of August.

Now adults, it was love at first sight for both.

He said he had never seen anyone so beautiful her golden hair glistening in the sun and she had never seen anyone so handsome. Her parents had immediately started their harangue of opposition to her marrying a fisherman. They felt she could do much better. After all they were the Parsons, an old southern family with fortunes earned by three generations in the shipping trades at the busy ports of New Orleans. Dr. Parsons didn't cotton to the heavy lifting required in the shipping business, even though the family had lackeys, it could still be arduous. Not for Charles Parsons. He chose psychiatry instead— sitting in a comfy brown leather chair talking to his patients lying on a couch. Excelling in the psychiatric profession, Dr. Parsons matched his ancestor's fortune and then some.

Doris Parsons had insisted her daughter be married on Anna Maria Island, a barrier island off the west coast of Florida. Doris had grown up on the island and wanted her daughter, the baby of the family, to feel her roots on this special day. Doris had asked a childhood friend, a snowbird who always flew north away from Florida's summer heat and humidity, if the bridal party could stay in her beach house while they prepared for the wedding. The dear friend insisted the Parson's take advantage of the house for the summer if they liked.

Patty Sue gazed out at the sparkling blue waves—three more nights and then she would be Mrs. Daniel Macintyre. "I'm so happy," she whispered. "Danny, I love you. Soon we'll be together—husband and wife." Her mind filled with her handsome groom. She could almost feel his arms tighten around her, folding her against his body.

Tapping her toe on the floor continuing the slow motion of the swing, she looked around. She would never be able to live in a house such as this. Her mother and father had spent hours explaining that she would live a hard life as the wife of a fisherman. They told her she would spend most of her hours alone while he was out at sea for days, perhaps weeks at a time, always in debt by several thousand dollars to pay for supplies before leaving the dock and landing his first fish. She would only know poverty.

Suddenly Patty Sue's nerves gripped her. She began to tremble. Dots of perspiration gathered on her forehead. Her breathing accelerated. She ran her hands up and down her arms. Her eyes sought the beautiful flower arrangement the girl had placed on the kitchen island—two colorful Birds of Paradise in the center, surrounded by blue iris and yellow and white lilies. It was a work of art. The crystal vase glistened in the filtered summer sun sending prisms of colorful rainbows around the room as the sun swept high in the sky.

But the bouquet didn't look right to Patty Sue. She stepped closer, reached for a blue iris. The vase tumbled. Crashed to the floor.

Patty Sue ran to the telephone by the computer set in a kitchen alcove, its screen magically filling with one picture after the other of the owner's travels, family, friends. The movement of fleeting pictures caused her head to spin.

"No! No!" she screamed.

Her skin crawled. Turned cold. Her stomach roiled, nauseous. Grasping the receiver, she stabbed at the numbers her hand sickeningly jerking before her. Certain she had hit the wrong numbers, she held her finger down on the button and tried again. But before she could dial the phone rang.

She jerked her finger away hearing the voice, biting her lip, tasting blood.

"Hi, there." The voice was calm, cool, in control.

"Thank God it's you. My nerves. I'm shaking. I need you. Help me. Please come. Hurry. You know where I am."

Chapter 2

Doris Parsons slapped the menu down for the third time, the fingernails on her right hand clicking impatiently on the table. "Where's my daughter? I shouldn't have left her. Probably telling Millie how *wonnnderful* Daniel is. Now Regina's missing. Marianne, where did Regina say she was going when she jumped off the trolley? She's been gone ... oh my heavens, almost an hour."

"Mrs. Parsons, I'll try Patty Sue again. Surely she'll pick up this time ... or she'll pop through the door." Marianne smiled reassuringly as she rose, walking quickly to the payphone inside the restaurant's entrance. Punching in the number for the beach house, she glanced up feeling Mrs. Parson's eyeballs. The phone ringing waiting to be answered, Marianne diverted her eyes to the tranquil beauty of the waves washing up on the beach, framed in the restaurant's bank of windows. Her eyes were drawn back to Mrs. Parsons staring at her.

Marianne shook her head, returning the ringing receiver to the hook. No answer. She dialed again then returned to the table sliding into her place next to Mrs. Parsons and the other two empty chairs.

"Well, let's eat," Mrs. Parsons snapped. "I'm ordering a martini. What would you like? We'll have a bite ... then hunt down those sisters."

"Daniel's a good person, Mrs. Parsons. Works hard. Dreams of buying a fleet of commercial fishing boats—"

"Falderal. Dreaming is all he does. Where is that waitress?"

Marianne looked around at the other patrons enjoying their lunch, then looked through the dining room's arched portal to the front entrance of the restaurant.

"How do you think Regina's handling this whole wedding thing, Marianne? Marianne."

"What?"

"I said, how do you think Regina's holding up? She fancied Daniel for herself you know. But then Daniel caught sight of Patty Sue … when she blossomed."

"Reg seems to be okay. A few remarks here and there when Danny took up with Patty Sue. I think it really sank in that she lost him when you and Dr. Parsons said you'd buy Patty Sue a house to live in. I guess Danny is still sleeping in his apartment."

"Well, of course, he's still in that dingy box. Charles and I are waiting … maybe Patty Sue will come to her senses before we purchase a house. A few days yet … perhaps she'll see the folly in marrying such a man.

"What can I bring you two ladies?" the perky waitress asked, her red lips spreading in a wide smile. She took their order including a double martini for Mrs. Parsons and instructions to watch for two more in their party … expected any moment.

"Go try to reach Patty Sue again, dear," Doris said with a sigh.

Marianne placed the call tapping her finger on the receiver in her hand counting the rings. Raising her brows she looked at Mrs. Parsons and shook her head. No answer.

"Do you have Daniel's number?" Mrs. Parsons asked as Marianne approached. "We can call him on the boat that is if his ship-to-shore phone is working. Seems like it conks out every day. Maybe Patty Sue called him. Maybe he knows where she is."

Marianne retrieved a little red address book from her tote, flicked through the pages to Danny's ship number and tapped the code.

Danny Macintyre, six-foot tall, muscular, leaned back against the winch holding the chains for the boat's anchor, watching the wake of his fishing vessel, the spew of water catching the sunbeams sending a fantasy of colored lights before his eyes. Patty Sue would be having lunch about now with her mom and her bridesmaids. He wished she was here with him, in his arms. How lucky he was. How thankful he had waited for his princess. His lips moved feeling her kiss. His eyes glazed as the beauty of his bride sent lightning bolts through his body.

The crew smiled seeing their skipper gazing out at the sparkling blue water. They were happy for him. He was a wonderful captain. Always concerned about their welfare, sharing everything he could from the sale of their catch.

They saw him walk to the wheelhouse, pick up the mike of the ship-to-shore phone.

They chuckled ... probably his bride calling to tell him she loved him. Since Danny had asked the blonde to marry him, they never seemed to be apart unless he was out in his boat which he had renamed *The Patty Sue* painted in dark blue on the vessel's white hull.

"The Patty Sue. Over."

"Hi, Danny. It's Marianne. By any chance has Patty Sue called you in the last hour or so?"

"No. I thought she was having lunch with you," he replied watching a pelican diving for his lunch.

"That was the plan. We left her at the beach house. She was waiting for the seamstress to make the final adjustments to her gown, but we haven't seen her. Regina either, for that matter."

Danny's brows drew together, the fantasy lights and pelican forgotten. "That's not like my Patty Sue. If you can't find her, if I don't hear from you in the next thirty minutes I'll head back.

"Okay," Marianne said.

Danny shook away the dread sneaking into his mind.

"I'll call you, if I find Patty Sue," Marianne repeated. "It's a beautiful day for fishing, Danny."

"It was. Hell, I'm heading in now. Where will you be?"

"Hang on a minute. Mrs. Parsons is here with me ... Danny, we'll meet you back at the beach house where we left Patty Sue. If you see Regina on your way, call us. We can't find her either."

"Okay," he muttered as he hung up.

The hair on the back of Danny's neck prickled as he turned the wheel heading northeast to Cortez. He and Patty Sue had decided he would pursue his business out of the old fishing village connected by a bridge to the southern tip of Anna Maria Island. The couple felt they needed to put some space between them and her family's continued harassment over their plans to marry. And were pleasantly surprised the day Mrs. Parsons insisted, if they were going marry, that the ceremony be performed on the island where she had grown up. Her friend's beach house would be a perfect place to relax as they made final arrangements for the wedding.

On Danny's next sojourn out into the Gulf he sprang the plan on his crew. Tired of New Orleans, they eagerly agreed to stay with him—new sights to see, new places to go, and new girls to conquer. Told all the crew that is except his dad. Danny had followed his father's love of the Gulf waters as a fisherman but was the first to own his own boat. His mom died of lung cancer, a chain smoker worrying while she waited for her husband to return from the sea. His dad occasionally crewed for him but more often than not would be found with his retired buddies, hanging out, swapping stories at the one of the bars near the docks of New Orleans.

However, when his dad learned his plans to fish out of Cortez, he quickly joined his son with new buddies on the Cortez docks. He also worried about his son's upcoming nuptials. He knew how hard it was for a wife left on land by her fisherman husband. He knew it was the root cause of his wife's death, along with his meager earnings. He had purchased a piece of land in Cortez. Land he had kept secret from his wife. She would have thought it frivolous. Money was needed elsewhere.

Danny pulled his green 1969 Ford pickup truck onto the red brick driveway of the beach house and parked behind a silver BMW. Frowning he jumped down out of the truck. The BMW belonged to Dr. Parsons who wasn't expected until Friday.

The garage door was open and Danny took the stairs up to the main floor two at a time calling out for Patty Sue.

"Well, Daniel, about time you got here." Dr. Parsons took one sniff of Daniel Macintyre and backed away in disgust. The fisherman hadn't even taken the courtesy of showering before galloping into their presence.

Ignoring Dr. Parsons, Daniel pushed by, locking eyes with Mrs. Parsons sitting in a straight chair, a hanky twisting in her hands.

Marianne rushed up to him clutching him with a fierce hug. "Danny, we can't find her. We can't find Regina either. It's been five hours."

"What do you mean you can't find Regina? I'm right here." Regina, dressed in tattered cutoff jeans, wet sneakers, a white stained shirt, looked at her mother and then her father who stepped away from her as he had Daniel. Regina was a blonde like her younger sister but the similarity ended there. Regina's features were chiseled like her mother's displaying none of Patty Sue's softness.

"Where in the name of heaven have you been?" Dr. Parsons snapped.

"Patty Sue is gone," Regina whispered turning to Danny, her eyes misting.

"What do you mean she's gone?" Danny jerked Regina's arm turning her in front of him.

"Oh, Danny, I don't know," her eyes filled with compassion. "I came back here to wait for her and she was gone … wedding dress on the closet floor." Regina confessed she had run north on the beach a mile to the city pier, the northern tip of the island. She thought for sure she would see her sister. Maybe she was having second thoughts.

Doris Parsons raced to the next room, yanked open the closet door. Gasping, she knelt to the floor gathering the creamy beaded chiffon to her cheeks.

Dr. Parsons and Daniel rushed through the bedroom door, Daniel pushing the doctor out of his way. Fear gripped the fisherman. A fear stronger than he had ever felt before. Stronger than any he had experienced in raging storms out at sea.

"She must have been kidnapped," Danny uttered, the words strangling in his throat.

It was almost midnight when he yanked the receiver off the hook in the kitchen and dialed 9-1-1.

By the next morning, the police told the Parsons and Daniel that they had found no trace of Patty Sue, no trace of a fight. No one had seen her after her mother and sister and Marianne had left the beach house to go to the restaurant. Mrs. Parsons dialed the seamstress. When asked, Millie said she did not go to the fitting. Patty Sue had called cancelling their appointment.

According to the police logs no crimes had been reported on Anna Maria Island in the last twenty-four hours. The police captain was very solicitous saying his officers would keep a look out, but he and his force, without evidence of foul play, had concluded that Patty Sue Parsons was a runaway bride.

Danny did not accept their conclusion.

He ran down the stairs, out of the beach house, Regina racing after him. The two of them stopped tourists on the street, entered establishments along Gulf Drive, the street running through the center of Anna Maria Island. Had anyone seen Patty Sue? He flashed her picture from his wallet in front of anyone who would listen.

No one had seen the pretty blonde.

They stopped trolley after trolley asking the conductors if they had seen the smiling woman in the picture in the last two days.

None had.

Marianne joined Danny and Regina as they contacted the car rental agencies, the taxi companies, and, a long shot, the bicycle rentals.

All dead ends.

They continued their efforts on Friday.

However, Dr. and Mrs. Parsons had agreed with the police conclusion that their daughter was a runaway bride. Maybe she had come to senses after all. They felt that Patty Sue would contact them soon. Perhaps she had returned to the family home in New Orleans.

Saturday, the morning they were to be married, Daniel Macintyre fingered the St. Christopher medal Patty Sue had given him. "This will keep you safe so you will always come home to me," she said. His head drooped as he caressed the medal. Then, pulling himself up, he slowly dressed in his tuxedo and left the little room he had rented for the Roser Memorial Chapel.

Holding a red rose, he walked up between the nine rows of church pews and sat on the plush carpeted step leading up to the altar. He sat facing the back of the church his eyes riveted on the door where he prayed his bride would enter.

Regina and Marianne sat beside Danny on the step in front of the altar. The Parsons sat shoulder to shoulder in the first pew on one side. The crew of The Patty Sue fishing vessel, including his dad, sat on the other side. The remaining eight rows of pews were vacant. The priest nervously paced back and forth in front of the altar, his long black robe, white collar and white gown fluttering at each turn in direction.

As the time approached for the ceremony, the Parsons, heads held high but faces tight with concern, yet believing their precious daughter would return, walked outside to turn away the few guests who had been invited, telling them the bride had been taken ill. There would be no wedding today.

The hour of the ceremony passed by.

Another hour passed.

"Danny, she's not coming," Regina whispered threading her hand through his arm.

He looked at her, his eyes welling with tears. Regina, holding his arm, urged him to stand. He saw his dad step from the pew into the aisle. Taking a few quick strides he grasped his son in a strong hug. "I'm so sorry, Danny," his father whispered. "You'll be back out to sea in a few days. The sea will give you strength, son."

The hug ended, arms dropping to their sides, and Regina walked the downcast groom out of the church into the blinding sunshine.

Marianne remained seated, watching as the pair retreated.

"Want to go to the Sandbar … a couple of blocks … have a drink?" Regina asked, her brown eyes filled with sympathy.

Danny nodded, yes.

The Parsons and Danny's fishing crew watched as Danny, slowly putting one foot in front of the other steadied by Regina's arm around his waist, walked away from the church.

Chapter 3

The Sandbar restaurant was busy, always busy with townies and tourists on a Saturday afternoon in the middle of summer. It was a perfect location for romance—the sun dipping in the west casting a golden glow over the waves lapping the shore of the island.

Heads turned as the handsome couple walked by. Regina, her long red gown clinging to her curves held in place by tiny spaghetti straps, led Danny to a cozy spot off to the side of the patio surrounded by bushy palms, the table legs anchored in deep, soft white sand. It was a secluded nook, a paradise for lovers, but not Danny. He was filled with thoughts of rejection. Regina ordered two Mai Tais with extra rum for her friend, and, yes, serve the drinks with a little umbrella perched to the side in the glass.

Danny, slumping in the white chair, leaned forward, elbows on the white table, head propped up in his hands, gazed at the water as the sun dipped below the horizon. Three days ago he was out fishing in those waters, full of anticipation and love for his bride. *How could I have been so wrong? I thought Patty Sue loved me. I believed her when she embraced our plans to move to this island. Her leaving me must be the work of her mother and father. They hate me, a fisherman. I bet they know where she is. They stole her from me.*

The drinks were served and Regina waved the waitress off. She sat quietly, resting her hand on Danny's arm—a friend supporting a friend in great pain. Danny lifted the umbrella from the stemmed glass, dropped it on the table and drained the icy liquid in three gulps.

Danny diverted his eyes from the wedding in progress a few yards away—a special event, the Sandbar was famous for their beach weddings. The bride was blonde, the groom tanned with black wavy hair ruffled by the soft breeze. The vows complete, the barefoot newlyweds walked through the few rows of barefoot guests sitting on white chairs. Stopping briefly at the end of the last row, the best man opened a black box filled with seashells. He handed a shell to each guest as they followed the blonde in the long white gown with her husband to the shore. The sleeves of the groom's white silk shirt fluttered as they hustled down to the water. Gathered at the edge of the sea, the guests made silent wishes for the newlyweds throwing their shells into the water with their blessings.

Danny swallowed hard. The couple could easily have been him and Patty Sue.

Regina, gently grasping his hand in hers, knew what he was thinking. Danny raised her hand to his lips. "Thank you, Regina, for rescuing me from the chapel, from your parents ... for staying with me."

The young waitress caught Regina's eye. Regina nodded, yes, another round.

"Did you see this coming, Regina? Your sister ... misgivings about marrying me?" Danny tossed the second tiny red umbrella from his glass to the side, took a long swallow praying something, anything, would help numb his pain.

"No, Danny, I never suspected. She seemed happy ... but she's really just a kid. Maybe she was more excited about being a bride than being your wife. There were times when she was a bundle of nerves, but what girl isn't when she's about to take the big step."

"You'd think she would have said something ... nothing. I was blindsided ... so pretty, so sweet." Danny waved at the waitress, circled his hand for another round.

Regina sat silently. *I would never have left this man. His body so full of passion. I'll show him that I'm the lover my sister was never capable of being.*

Two more drinks were served, umbrellas tossed to the side. Regina asked the waitress for two plastic cups of water they could take with them giving the young girl a large bill, pushing it into her hand to keep the change, indicating they wanted to be left alone.

"Danny, let's take our drinks, walk along the beach. We can talk … away from all these people, the noise of the band."

Regina emptied the water cups on the sand beside her chair filling them with the new drinks. "Come on. Here, take my hand." Leaning against him, they stood a moment. She took a step. Danny dutifully took a step with her, then another. Anyone seeing the pair would have taken them for lovers, lovers who only had eyes for each other, lovers fading from view.

Up a ways on the sandy beach was a clump of low bushes bordering the property line of a cottage. Regina sat on the warm sand pulling Danny down beside her.

Taking the now empty drink from his hand she offered him a sip from her cup. He laid back, looking up as the stars began to twinkle in the deepening gray to black sky. Regina nestled close to his body. He raised his arm welcoming her, cradling her next to him. Turning her eyes to his, splaying her hand on his cheek, she slowly wove her fingers through his hair. Rolling against his chest she softly traced his face, then gently touched her lips to his.

"Danny, I never told you that I love you. I've loved you for years. I had hoped one day … but you chose my little sister." Regina again brushed his lips with hers. He responded pulling her body closer, raising his mouth to hers.

"Regina, I didn't know … Patty Sue never said … you?"

Regina silenced him with another kiss warmer than the last. "Patty Sue left you, Danny. I will never do that. I will love you forever."

Danny rolled over holding her hands to the side of her head, looking down, one leg over hers. "Patty Sue—"

"Patty Sue left you, Danny. But I'm here. I love you. This is your wedding night, Danny. Love me. Love me, now."

Straining against his hands holding hers now above her head, pent up heat sprang through his body, his kisses turned urgent. Freeing her hands, his became hot, roaming her curves, hot curves of a woman loving him, wanting him, moaning in response to his touch, his desire, his need, urging him on.

Chapter 4

The crew of The Patty Sue watched as their skipper morphed into a surly, who-cares-how-I-treat-you man. He was rude. Barked orders. Forbidden in the past, he brought beer and liquor onboard, drinking the hours away while they toiled to haul in the catch. At times he let the men join him at the end of the day, but most days he finished off a six-pack, then two, starting on the third by the time they pulled into the slip.

Regina was always at the dock waiting for him to return.

Around the end of October Danny surprised his crew. He told them to drop anchor, inviting them to join him in a celebration. Regina was pregnant and they were going to elope the next day. They were not going to wait to suffer the wrath of her parents.

When Patty Sue ran away, Dr. Parsons reneged on his promise to pay for the repairs needed to keep Danny's fishing trawler operating, but Regina didn't miss a beat. Spitting venom at her father, she told him she was marrying Daniel Macintyre. They didn't need her father's money. On her twenty-fifth birthday she could get her hands on the trust her grandfather had left her. She would support Danny, pay off the loan on his boat that her father had promised to pay after Patty Sue married him. Dr. Parsons, however, made good on one offer he had made to his daughter—he bought the newlyweds a small bungalow in the Cortez fishing village. Good riddance. He wanted them out of New Orleans.

Danny's drinking continued. His crew, fearful of losing their jobs, picked up the slack and kept the meager revenue coming in spite of Danny's decline.

The following April Danny was at the helm out in the Gulf watching his crew pull up a net full of shrimp when the radio sounded an incoming call. It was Regina. She had gone into labor and was crying for him to meet her at the hospital. She was in extreme pain.

The gear was quickly stowed and Danny headed The Patty Sue back to Cortez. Climbing off the boat the crew urged Danny to stop and have a celebratory drink with them. He was going to be a father.

Danny reasoned that Regina wouldn't be having the baby quickly, so he obliged.

An hour and four beers later he left the gang. They slapped him on the back as he exited the bar into the waning daylight.

A baby. Patty Sue had talked about having a baby. Their baby. Thinking about his sweetheart, Danny drove over the bridge onto Anna Maria Island, swung left to a deserted spot on the beach and parked. Retrieving a flask from under the seat of his truck, he jumped down and strolled through the marshy grass to the soft sand and the lapping waves. He was sure there was plenty of time to get to the hospital before the big event.

Evening dissolved into night as Danny staggered along the beach. Someone after an afternoon of sunbathing had left a beach chair so he sat down … for just a minute.

It was a balmy April night. A cloud skittered overhead partially covering the moon. Off in the distance he saw a woman wearing a white dress. She was slowly walking toward him. Squinting, he couldn't quite make her out, but as she came closer he could see her blond hair. She was wearing a wedding dress. Strange to see someone strolling on the beach in her wedding … a chill enveloped him … she was so close.

"Hello, Danny."

"Patty Sue, is that you?" he whispered.

"Yes, it's me."

"You're crying. Why are you crying?"

"I miss you, Danny."

"Oh, I miss you too, Patty Sue. I've been so miserable … out in the water I dream about you … but—"

"I know, my love. I must go now."

"My darling, wait …

"I'll see you again."

"See me again ... you are so beautiful." Danny waved his arm, tried to touch her, but felt only a light breeze ... the scent of gardenias ... her scent.

"I will watch over you and your son. Take care of little Mac, Danny. I will help."

"Mac? Wait ... don't leave me ... Patty Sue." Danny struggled to his feet. Patty Sue was walking away... dissolving ... vanishing. He ran down the beach calling to her but it was no use. She was gone. Out of breath he stumbled to his truck fear gripping him. He was sure he was losing his mind. "I have to go to the hospital ... the hospital ... our baby," he mumbled.

Within twenty minutes he entered the Manatee Memorial Hospital, miraculously feeling none of the alcohol he had consumed. The attendant at the information desk directed him to the maternity ward, the nursery.

Regina had given birth to a nine-pound baby boy.

Stopping in front of the glass, looking into the bassinets holding the babies, Danny saw the name Macintyre. To spite Regina's father, they had decided to name the newborn Charles after him.

The baby was crying, his fists quivering in the air. He was going to be a man to be reckoned with. Danny smiled at his son waving his clenched fist, returning the greeting.

Danny felt a nudge on his arm. It was his dad grinning from ear to ear. "I hear you're a father. Which one?" he asked.

Danny smiled. "There, Dad. The baby raising his fists in the air."

"Oh, he's a strong boy, son. A fisherman for sure."

The nurse motioned to the men at the window that she was bringing the baby to his mother to be fed.

Danny turned, strolled down the hall to find Regina, his dad following stride for stride eager to meet his grandson.

The birth had been hard. Regina vowed never to have another child. She whispered to the infant suckling at her breast that he, Charles Daniel Macintyre, would protect her, adore her, and only her for as long as she lived.

Part Two
Chapter 5

Thirty-six years later – Bradenton, Florida

Angry, black storm clouds disgorged sheets of rain flooding the roads of Florida's West Coast. A siren screamed in the early morning hour from an EMT van slicing through the thunder and lightning as it raced from Cortez to Bradenton along palm-tree-lined streets, their fronds giving way to forty-miles-per-hour winds. The broad, black tires spewed water in their wake as the white vehicle raced to Manatee Memorial Hospital.

The patient lost consciousness as the medics cut away his bloody shirt and applied a tourniquet trying to stem the flow of blood from his mangled left arm, his pulse fluttering.

The van pulled to a stop under the portico of the hospital's emergency entrance alongside another ambulance delivering two victims from a car that had careened off a slick highway. Interns hauling a rolling gurney rushed out the sliding plate-glass doors and up to the van. The EMTs flung open the van's back doors calling out the condition of their patient as they transferred the unconscious, blood-soaked man onto the gurney. The interns, two on either side, grasped the rails and quickly retreated through the open doors, down the hall into the blinding white emergency operating room.

Dr. Grayson took one look at the unconscious man as the gurney approached the operating table, holding her gloved hands in the air away from her green scrubs as her patient was transferred onto the table.

The briefing from the EMTs on the van had been detailed: white male, commercial fisherman, an accident on his vessel brought on by the storm's crashing waves in the Gulf. Bone visible through the gash in his arm. Significant loss of blood.

Could she save the arm? Hell, could she save the man?

She yelled questions, orders: "Hemoglobin count? Blood type? X-ray left arm, crash cart ready, stat."

The operating team covered in scrubs from head to toe, doctors in green, nurses in blue. Scrub caps were tied around their heads, white masks over nose and mouth. Only their eyes were visible, trained on their patient, responding in precision to the surgeon's orders.

"Hemoglobin 7, BP 49," a nurse shouted.

"Blood type?" Grayson demanded.

"O-negative," another nurse answered.

"Blood ready?"

"Four pints."

"We're losing him," Grayson shouted as the monitor flat lined. "Paddles!"

"Clear," the anesthesiologist responded, then applied the paddles to the man's upper torso.

"Again," Grayson demanded.

"Clear." The body jerked in response to the volts of electricity.

Grayson watched the monitor. "Come on, big guy. Come on ... come on ... yes!" She expelled the air she held in her lungs seeing the blip on the monitor.

The man's heart registered a beat, another, and another. Erratic, but it was beating.

"Blood. Two units. Now," Grayson demanded. Her voice strong, in control, no hesitation. This was her world. She was in charge. She was their leader.

The fisherman lying unconscious on the metal table was probably in his thirties, muscular from years of casting the lines, hauling the nets, pulling the heavy loads of fish onto the deck. Dr. Grayson took all into account and prayed his rugged body would pull him through the trauma he had suffered this day. The upper arm bone showing through the open wound was not broken but there were tears to the tendons and muscle. Looking away from the X-rays projected on the screen, Grayson bent over her patient.

Surgery began.

The man's pulse was thready as she started the process of repairing, of trying to save his arm. Grayson ordered a transfusion of two additional units of blood.

Miraculously, the fisherman's heartbeat grew stronger as the operation proceeded.

You are a fine specimen of a man, my friend, the doctor thought. *Keep up the fight!*

At mid-day Dr. Grayson in a pair of fresh green scrubs, stopped by the Intensive Care Unit to check on her patient. Three men dressed in heavy rubber boots, their shirts stained with blood, stood peering through the window in the doorway of the ICU. The doctor surmised they were friends of the man she had operated on earlier, more than likely his crew who had stepped up as first responders administering to their captain when he was injured.

"Excuse me," Dr. Grayson said nudging past the men.

"Oh, excuse us, ma'am. Do you know how Mac is?"

"Mac?"

"Yes, Captain Charles Macintyre, our skipper. We call him Mac. He's the man over there in the second bed. The nurse said we could look but we couldn't go in."

"Captain Macintyre survived a significant loss of blood but seems stable at the moment. I'm not sure how much he'll be able to use his—"

"Oh, don't you worry, ma'am. If it's attached, Mac will see that it works. Are you his nurse?"

"I'm Dr. Grayson. I operated on your friend."

"Wow, think of that, Studs, a lady Doc. Excuse my manners, ma'am. This here is Studs, and Shrimp, I'm Sissy. Them's not our real names, but what we go by. If you get a chance, you tell Mac, that Studs, Shrimp and Sissy came to see him."

Dr. Grayson's eyes crinkled with merriment at the three. Studs, staring at her, was the shorter one of the three, a handsome, pretty man, with sandy hair to his shoulders and a tattoo of an arrow piercing a heart peeking out from under the sleeve of his orange T-shirt. Grayson didn't know it yet but Studs thought all women were beautiful especially the doc standing in front of him, her auburn hair circling around her shoulders.

Shrimp, a black man, was taller than the other two. He had a nasty scar on his calf from a shark bite, barely visible beneath his rolled-up jeans. Sissy, Asian, a scar across his face, was not a man she would want to tangle with. His body looked almost as tough as the man she had operated on. Both wore tattered heavy green pants topped with yellow T-shirts stained with their leader's blood.

"Well, gentlemen, let me check if your Captain is awake and up to visitors. Mind you, it would have to be brief—hello and goodbye."

Chapter 6

The big man in bed two squinted in the dim light. He watched his crew of three trying unsuccessfully to keep their balance, tippy-toeing in rubber boots that didn't cooperate, falling against one another as they left the room.

Smiling after the men, Dr. Grayson removed the clipboard hanging from the end of the fisherman's bed: thirty-six, six-foot-two, two-hundred-twenty-one pounds, eyes brown. *Big brown eyes*, she thought glancing up at him noting the thick black hair grazing his shoulders. Even though his body was covered with a white sheet, his damaged arm lying limp on top, he exuded more testosterone than any male patient she'd seen after such an operation. Most appeared weak but not this one. There was no check box on the form for square jaw, permanent five o'clock shadow or Charles Macintyre's testosterone level.

The fisherman looked away from his crew stumbling out the door to the woman scanning the chart at the foot of his bed. He tried to move a finger and felt a stab of pain for his efforts. "Nurse, what's on that clipboard? I don't feel so hot," his voice groggy, barely audible. He tried unsuccessfully to raise his arm covered with a white compression sleeve over the wound to control the swelling from his wrist to above the dressing.

"Well, you're awake," she said smiling. "That's a good sign, Captain Macintyre. I'm Dr. Grayson. I performed your surgery. You may not 'feel so hot' but you look a lot better than you did a few hours ago."

Mac closed his eyes. *A lady doctor, a surgeon. Can't tell what she looks like in that garb except it's obvious she's a woman.* His lids rose, then closed. He fought the anesthetic to keep his eyes open. "Doc, call me Mac. So, what's the verdict? Sleep here tonight … join my crew tomorrow?"

"I don't think tomorrow is in the cards." Grayson replaced the clipboard at the end of the bed and stepped to his right side, his good arm. Putting her fingers on his wrist, looking at her watch, she monitored his pulse. It was strong as was the tanned, weather-beaten arm. Taken with his strength, she put her skilled, delicate surgeon's hand in his large palm feeling the calloused skin, understanding how hard it was for him to lay helpless.

"The gash in your arm required sixty-three stitches inside and forty-seven outside to repair the damage." she said softly, laying his hand back on the sheet.

"You count the stitches?" His lips turned up slightly but even that seemed to shoot pain down his left arm.

"It's part of your record. You have a compression sleeve covering your arm, the dressing over your wound. I ordered morphine in your drip, the needle in the top of your hand, to keep you comfortable. Are you comfortable?"

"Groggy. I can't feel all those stitches … maybe a few." He tried to smile again. It was weak, but Grayson saw the attempt and took it as a good sign.

"Groggy is good. You were given four units of blood. We'll check your hemoglobin in the morning. You may need another pint."

"What's with the hemoglobin thing?" He tried to turn his body but again electric waves shot through his left side stopping the attempt.

"Well, a count of eleven is wonderful. Last count you were a seven."

"How long do I have to wear this white thing?"

"A couple of weeks. Keeps the dressing in place but more important keeps the swelling down. AND you can't get the dressing wet."

"Well, you'll have to tell me how I'm going to manage to keep it dry because I'll be out on my boat long before that. My crew is good, tough as you saw, but I have to be with them. No work no pay. I could lose The Regina."

"Regina?"

"My boat—my mother's name. Hey ... where's my Saint Christopher medal? Protects me. Probably saved my life. Damn winch ripped my arm ... could have just as easily ripped my throat." The fingers on his right hand were searching through his thick, black chest hairs.

"No jewelry, Captain, during your stay with us. But I'll check the safe. Everything we took off you, ah, your jewelry, is in the safe. Your clothes were soaked with blood. I'm afraid they were discarded."

Mac's right hand flopped to his thigh feeling the soft white cloth of the sheet next to his skin. "All of them?"

"Yes, sir. All of them," the doctor chuckled.

"I need a cigarette. Can you get me one?"

Grayson chuckled again.

Mac's eyes found her face. Maybe he was dying. Her laugh was musical, like he imagined an angel's would be. But angels had blond hair he was told. This lady surgeon's hair was dark brown, with ... with what ... auburn streaks. He was definitely in worse shape than he thought. Auburn? How did he know that color?

"I think not today, Captain. I ordered a patch ... your right arm. Help you with the nicotine craving. You might take this opportunity to give up smoking."

"No way, Doc." Mac's lids drooped. "Not a chance. How'd you know I smoke?"

"Oh, I have ways. Besides, we found an empty pack in your shirt pocket."

"You said I can't get out of here tomorrow. What about the next day?"

"I'll see you in the morning, check your hemoglobin ... *thing*. We'll have a better idea then. Sleep tight, Captain," Grayson whispered.

Her patient's chin dropped, his breathing soft and rhythmic. The big guy was in la-la land.

Chapter 7

Dr. Grayson stepped briskly through the white hall to check on the fisherman before leaving the hospital for the day. She quietly entered his room now in shadows. Checking his pulse a smile played over her full lips. All things considered he was doing very well.

Turning to leave she felt a sudden chill and pulled her white cotton coat together as the chill enveloped the room. She turned back the chill continuing up her arms. The sheet had slipped revealing the captain's curly black chest hairs.

Mac's eyes fluttered, his fingers clutching at his heart.

His mouth opened.

He gasped for air.

"Can't breathe," he said in a raspy whisper to the woman hovering over him in a long white gown. She touched his forehead. Kissed his brow. Mac tried to touch her. The white vision evaporated. His right hand lifted slightly off the sheet, brow scrunching as he tried to speak. "Who?" he whispered. His mouth open, his tongue pressed to his teeth. The word *thanks* ... rode the air over his lips.

Grayson knew immediately what was happening to her patient—a reaction to the morphine, the IV drip, drop by drop entering his body. She hit the emergency button at the same time removing the drip.

Gail, an intern assigned to him, rushed into the room. "The emergency light ... what happened?"

"Morphine reaction. Get the narcotic antagonist and a fresh drip bag, stat." Grayson barked the order as she removed his pillow, bending his neck back to allow as much air as possible to enter his lungs.

Gail ran back into the room holding out the fresh drip setup to the doctor.

Grayson deftly stuck the IV needle into his lower right arm releasing several doses of the antidote directly into the captain's body at the same time noticing a number of red dots on his upper arm. Hives. Another indication of a reaction to the morphine he had been administered for pain. Watching the second hand sweep around the clock over his bed, at two minutes she released another surge of the antidote.

Mac's breathing began to ease.

Grayson continued to monitor the sweep of the second hand. At another two minutes, she released an additional intravenous dose thwarting the morphine reaction.

In her peripheral vision she saw Mac's fingers curl slightly into his palm. His breathing was now even, rhythmic. His brow eased.

Who was she, the woman in a long white dress? He tried to touch his forehead feeling for the kiss but the doctor had hold of his wrist. He turned his head to the doc. She was fussing with something he couldn't see. *Dr. Grayson is wearing a white coat. I must have been mistaken.*

Doctor Grayson relaxed. Her patient was going to be all right. She shivered thinking of what might have happened if she had not been in the room, had not felt chilled, had not turned back. Looking at him he was staring, looking at her as if for the first time. She felt his eyes caressing her face. The chill she had felt when the episode began was gone. Her skin felt warm. She touched Mac's hand checking the IV drip. His hand was warm to her touch.

Mac's lips drew up slightly. A smile. A soft sigh escaped his mouth as his eyes closed.

Grayson expelled a quiet sigh, as she closed her eyes thanking God her patient had fought off a fatal reaction and that she was in the room to catch it.

Chapter 8

The gray PT Cruiser traced over I-4 heading west to Tampa then south to their destination. Elizabeth Stitchway, a perpetual smile on her face, raised her ring finger off the steering wheel the diamond catching the sun, radiating rainbows. Gripping the wheel again she stole a quick glance at her Aunt Jane and lovingly patted her hand. The seventy-two year old woman's lips bowed in return, her silver hair glowed with a hint of pink accentuating her apple cheeks and merry blue eyes.

Maggie, Elizabeth's black and white Border collie mix, slept in the back of the car—plenty of room with the seatback laid flat for the dog and Aunt Jane's cat, GumDrop.

Aunt Jane always took GumDrop with her after a twister tore down her street leaving nothing but rubble. GumDrop went missing for three days returning with cuts on her paws. Aunt Jane went straight to Wal-Mart and bought a large carrier for her companion.

At first Maggie's nose was out of joint with the little orange intruder, but now they were pals. GumDrop was asleep on her back, four paws in the air flopping over at her furry ankles, her nose protruding a notch through a hole in the carrier.

Liz thought how lucky she was to have Aunt Jane, always up for a new adventure. Jane and her late husband Mortimer Haliday had squirreled away a fortune investing their salaries in Apple computer stock when it first went on the market, and buying gold bars before the prized metal had its big run up. Aunt Jane was worth a million several times over. She could live anywhere, but preferred to stay in the development of manufactured homes with her friends, especially Mabel her hair dresser.

"Aunt Jane, check the map. I marked a dog park where Manatee Avenue crosses over the bridge to Anna Maria Island. After three hours in the car I want to let Maggie run ... ten minutes anyway. We can stretch our legs, too. I marked an *X* for the motel. We'll register, get GumDrop and Maggie settled, then we'll check out the Sandbar ... just up the beach from the motel. I think they'll be okay in the room for a little while don't you?"

"A couple of hours, certainly. But then we have to spend some time with them."

"Sounds like a plan."

"Did you make an appointment with the event planner at the Sandbar about getting married on their beach?"

"No. I wanted to see it first, get a feel for the place before opening that discussion."

Two pairs of feet, toes painted with mango nail polish wiggled through the soft white sand as Jane and Liz sauntered arm in arm up to the Sandbar restaurant. Their sandals were stashed in rainbow-colored totes swinging from their shoulders. The totes emblazoned with: *Anna Maria Island, My Paradise in the Sun* were purchased at the gift shop next to the motel. Jane's calf-length dress covered with red poppies on a yellow field matched Liz's red shorts and yellow T-shirt. Matching colors except for their hair—Jane's silver pink and Liz's short red curls.

"Aunt Jane, look. There's the Sandbar. Oh, it's so pretty." Liz exclaimed squeezing Jane's arm with hers.

Jane looked up at her niece's beaming face. "Come on, dear. Strutting in the sand I've a thirst for a drink of iced tea. There, let's sit at that table in front under the white umbrella. No need to put on our sandals ... the table legs are stuck in the sand," she said chuckling.

Liz paused, looked up at the sun and then at the sparkling blue water, the Gulf of Mexico. *Manny's going to love this*, she thought. Turning in a circle to see the possibility of their wedding from every angle, she caught sight of the pavilion for wedding receptions that was featured on the website. It's white tent-like roof held up by large white pillars was separated for privacy from the restaurant by tall bushes.

While Liz was twirling about, Jane hustled to the table before someone else sat down. Her feet were tired from trudging through the sand. She nodded to a woman sitting alone next to a bush, her table to the side of the one Jane had spotted. "Your ice tea looks mighty refreshing," Jane said grinning.

The woman stared back, a half smile on her lips indicating she agreed with Jane's assessment as Jane ordered two ice teas and fish-of-the-day sandwiches.

Liz darted up to the table, sand flipping in the air with each step. "This is perfect, Aunt Jane."

Settled at the table, totes on the sand leaning against their chairs, sunglasses pushed high on their noses, the pair gazed out over the beach at the waves gently running to and fro.

A waitress, her white T-shirt tucked into a short black skirt, smiled as she rushed by. "I'll be right back with your sandwiches and tea orders."

"Isn't this beautiful?" Liz said glancing around at the beach and the covered patio behind them. "I think this will be a lovely setting to become a wife. Wife. Whoa. Can you believe it? I'm getting married." Liz lifted her diamond to her lips. Dear Manny. How she loved her police captain.

The waitress brought their lunch saying she'd check back, or to wave if they wanted something. Jane squeezed the juice from the lemon wedge on the side of the glass and took a long sip, a sprig of mint tickling her nose.

Liz pulled two pages from her tote she had printed off the Sandbar's website laying them on the table between them. "Here are some pictures of weddings that took place here. Just look at that sunset against this bride's white gown. Manny's bigger than this groom and much more handsome don't you think?"

Jane laughed. "Manny is definitely more handsome and you, Lizzie, are prettier than that bride—your red hair, or, are you going blonde?"

"Aunt Jane, the blonde was only that one time when I was undercover working on your case—Uncle Morty's stolen diamond bracelet."

"I knew having a professional private investigator in the family was going to come in handy. I just didn't appreciate how handy until you solved the case."

"*Manny* and I solved the case," Liz said patting her aunt's hand.

Jane felt someone staring at her. Turning she caught the eye of the same woman she had spoken to earlier. Now, taking a closer look, Jane guessed they were about the same age, seventy something.

The woman's floppy straw hat was ringed with roses mixed with daisies. She smiled back at Jane. Several strands of brightly colored beads sparkled as they cascaded down the woman's flowered sundress which flowed to her ankles. Purple toes peeked out from under the hem. The woman picked up her glass of iced tea and, taking a couple of steps, stood beside Jane. "Excuse me. You're planning a wedding." It wasn't a question, more of a statement as she glanced from Liz to Jane and back to Liz.

"Yes. Well, my niece is. What do you think of this place for a wedding? A small wedding … would you say about twelve, Lizzie?"

"Around that. Maybe a few more." Liz stood and extended her hand. "My name is Elizabeth Stitchway and this is my Aunt, Jane Haliday. Will you join us?"

The cherubic woman, no more than five feet, smiled. "Love to, dearie. My name is Madame Crystal."

Liz quickly pulled the woman's chair from her table situating it next to Jane as the waitress hustled up. "Madame Crystal, you've made new friends I see. More tea, ladies?"

"That would be lovely, Katie," Madame Crystal said. "And would you bring us each a little dish of sherbet—three different colors, please?"

"Of course, Crystal." Katie bustled off with a wink at her.

"Which are you going to choose, May, June, or September for your wedding, Elizabeth?"

"Madame Crystal—"

"Please call me Crystal. I only begin with Madame for my business."

Jane's brows shot up. "A business. How exciting. What business? Something we can buy?" Jane asked.

"If you like," Crystal giggled, a soft musical sound floating through her pink bowed lips. "I give readings."

"You're an author?" Liz asked.

"Oh, no. I'm a psychic. You can come to my home. I'll read your palm, but my specialty is Psychometry and the paranormal."

"I know of reading palms, tarot cards, but never heard of ... of that other word," Jane said

"I have, Crystal. Psychometry is when you hold a person's possession in your hand—you can tell things, see things about that person?"

"That's right, Elizabeth." Madame Crystal glanced around to see if anyone was in earshot. Satisfied there was no one, she leaned in, "I've even helped the police."

"Oh my, Crystal. You must be *very* psychic," Jane giggled. "I mean good at fortune telling."

"Crystal, why did you ask about the months I'm considering for my wedding?"

"Well, it just came to me ... May, June, September ... is there another?"

"Yes, August. But Manny, my fiancé, is the only one I've discussed the date with. Not even Aunt Jane."

"It's obvious, Lizzie. Crystal knows all. You'd better be careful, or better yet, when you're working on a case we can come see Crystal for help." Jane beamed at her new psychic friend.

"You see, when I heard you say wedding those three months popped in my head. I would have steered you away from August. That is if you are planning to be wed here on the island and from the looks of that piece of paper you must fancy the Sandbar."

"You're right, Crystal," Liz said looking wistfully at the surf twinkling in the bright sun. "It couldn't be more perfect." Looking back at Crystal's dark blue eyes staring at her from under the straw hat, one of the roses lifted from the brim on a whiff of air. "But why not August?"

"Many years ago a bride, well a bride-to-be, vanished three days before she was to be married. Her fiancé was heartbroken. He went to the church, sat in front of the altar waiting, hoping she would show up."

Crystal took a sip of tea setting her glass to the side as Katie placed the sherbets in front of the three ladies ... strawberry for Liz, orange for Jane, and lime for Crystal. Madame Crystal immediately shuffled the dishes: lime to Liz, strawberry to Jane, and orange for herself. Liz shot a glance at her aunt. Both shrugged their shoulders at the shift in colors.

"But she didn't show up, the bride?" Jane asked scooping a spoonful of her strawberry sherbet.

"No. Everyone said she was a run-away bride … you know, like the movie. But this bride didn't ever show up. Tragic."

Chapter 9

Summer hit northern Mexico with a vengeance—stifling heat and humidity left a person dripping in sweat within minutes. The small town that bordered Texas particularly felt the high temperature. Rather, some felt it. The poor felt it, especially the gun runners—the corredores de fusil lived out in the heat. The drug lords felt nothing in their air-conditioned haciendas.

Such was the case of the Camacho DelaCruz family.

The heir to the family business, Camacho DelaCruz's only son, Camacho DelaCruz, Jr. had been groomed for his succession to take over the operation: the best schools in Mexico, and Aeronautical Engineering Bachelor's and Master's degrees from MIT in the United States attending on an American Student Visa.

The son, born an albino, was affectionately called Junior. The irony of the name was lost on no-one. He was anything but a Junior. Tough as his father, no one dared to cross him, no one dared to challenge him. Family members were loyal to Junior. His demeanor, his brilliance, and his education proved he was superior, the one to lead the family, the one to take over from his ailing father. Loyalty also came from fear. Many feared his white hair, white skin, and pink eyes believing he had mystical powers.

The ring of the phone bounced off the tile floors hushed from one room to the next by the Oriental and Aubusson rugs. Irritated by the ringing in his ears, Junior snapped up the phone.

"Junior, that you?"

The voice was muffled, disguise, but Junior knew who it was. "I told you never to call me on this phone," he hissed into the receiver.

"We got trouble. We—"

"Stop! Call me on my cell."

"You ain't answering. I left messages."

"I'll answer!" Junior slammed the receiver down, strode out the doors to the patio, across the tile path lined with hibiscus bushes, through the archway to the back of the property. His cell vibrated. Jamming his fist into his pocket he pulled the device to his ear.

"Junior? You there?" the voice whispered.

"Yeah. Now, what's so important that you call during siesta? The family is here."

"THE family or your family."

"None of your business. Talk."

"You're in trouble. Could be BIG trouble."

"Wally, I said talk or do I replace you?"

"Arturo Perez's surgeon hired a lawyer to look into the old man's death."

"That was two years ago. Why now and why would he stir up trouble? Police could be called in and that's the last thing the Perez family would want."

"How should I know?" Wally wined. "Ever since Arturo ... since his death, they have come on hard times. When you lose the head of a family like that, without reprisal, members of the family think you're weak. I've talked to a few. They scattered. You know, Junior, some joined your family, the DelaCruz family."

"I strongly question your information. I don't get what Arturo's surgeon making a big ruckus has to do with me?"

"I'll tell you what it has to do. He found the woman ... the doctor who saw you ... you know ... saw *you*."

"Impossible. Besides, there were no questions ... she saw nothing. If she had, you would have heard. What's her name?"

"Maria Grayson. Doctor Maria Grayson," Wally whispered.

"Never heard of her. Now, keep your mouth shut and eyes open. Are you still assigned to the ICU floor at the Tulane hospital?" Junior asked.

"Assigned to another department months ago, but I'm back on the floor now. No one keeps the place as clean as I do," Wally said chuckling.

"Try to make contact with someone on the lawyer's staff. Find out for sure what he's up to. What he and that surgeon think they know."

"I will, Junior. You know you can count on me."

"Wally, there are two more men coming to your house. Should be in New Orleans by tonight. One needs treatment. He was shot as he surfaced from the Rio Grande River. Not bad, he says. Just grazed. He's one of my top men heading to Florida to steal more people from the Perez operation. Tell him to call me after you have a look."

"Okay, I'll take care of him, Junior."

"Where's the woman ... do you know?"

"Florida, I think. Some hospital."

"Find her! I doubt she saw anything. But, if she did then she has to be dealt with."

Junior had to think. So he did what he always did when he was puzzling through a situation. He saddled up Devil, his black stallion, and took off through the hills of Ciudad Juárez, up, up, up the rocky earth to a ledge that overlooked his family's vast property. His black clothing protecting his white skin from the sun. A black kerchief covered his nose, mouth and neck. Dark glasses covered his pink eyes under a wide-brimmed black hat.

"Why would Juan Perez, Arturo's only son, allow the family's surgeon to bring attention to the Perez family?" Junior asked his steed. "Juan is weak. He's an American citizen by birth but his family's roots are in Mexico."

Retrieving a fresh bottle of water from his saddlebag, Junior drained the warm liquid.

That woman ... she only saw my back, he mused. *She couldn't identify me if they tortured her. But I caught sight of her turning away from the door ... I can't take a chance. Our gun running operation is beginning to work like a well-oiled machine. The drug cartel never missed a beat when my family, the DelaCruz family, the biggest, most powerful family on the Mexican border, took over the Perez operation.*

The decision made, Junior slowly descended the hills letting the stallion pick his way through the rocks.

Now is not the time to falter. Our crusade has just begun. The surface-to-air missiles will be ready in a couple of months. Stupid Americans thinking that an unmanned drone will stop me.

Junior chuckled. He could see the headlines on the internet, on the front page of the El Paso Times, on cable news: UNMANNED MISSILE BRINGS DOWN UNMANNED DRONE.

"I'll beat the Americans at their own game beginning in Texas then Arizona. The DelaCruz family is coming. The fight will be joined. Americanos, your southern border is doomed. And that is just the beginning."

Spurring Devil, the pair flew down the remaining hillside, then across his land, Devil's black mane waving in the wind as was his masked rider's long white hair.

Chapter 10

Mac wanted out of the hospital.

Yeah, his arm hurt, throbbed like the devil. Doc Grayson said he required two transfusions during his surgery because of all the blood he lost, but he felt as strong as a barracuda. Even though his blood matched his pop's they had to go to the blood bank not daring to use Danny's with all his drinking, and who knew what else he had flowing through his veins.

Then there was his mother. Regina had the annoying habit of popping into his hospital room at odd hours. Mac didn't like being a captive audience for his mother and her constant harangue about his pop's drinking and gambling. He'd had enough as a kid growing up never knowing if his pop had a boat that day to go out fishing, or lost it in a poker game, or bought it back because he got lucky the night before. More often than not Mac had to hustle a job on another fishing vessel.

Daniel Macintyre was a joke around the docks. Once he had big night and the next day bought two boats. Unfortunately, the following week he lost one of the boats in another round of poker. Whatever boat he had it was old and in need of repair. His son, Mac, became a master at patching up the relics for another day out in the Gulf.

Mac became the real captain after his second year of law school, around his twenty-first birthday, when one day his pop didn't show up at the dock. Frustrated, Mac took the helm, barked the orders. Over time he had replaced his pop's crew with Studs, Shrimp, and Sissy. As a team they kept the Macintyre and Son business afloat, so to speak.

Mac left the name, The Regina, on the hull. He didn't care what they called her as long as her engine turned over and the fish were running: grouper, red snapper, and mullet.

"Dang it, where's the Doc?" he yelled at a nurse passing his door. She shrugged her shoulders and kept on walking. The man in 405 was getting crankier by the minute.

Mac threw his legs over the side of the bed his johnny shirt hiking up just as Dr. Grayson walked in. Suddenly embarrassed, an unaccustomed feeling for him, he quickly clawed at the flowered fabric and slid back on the bed pulling the sheet to cover his body.

Laughing, the doctor picked up his chart hanging at the end of the bed scanning the entries with her finger while trying to stifle another grin at her patient's discomfort.

"Well, Captain Macintyre, I hear you're getting restless."

"It's Mac, remember?"

"Oh, yes, well, given your state of disarray as I walked in, maybe you'd feel more comfortable calling me Maria … Mac." Maria smiled, perched on the side of the bed, and took in the man sitting in front of her. He was a far cry from the unconscious patient she had first seen. A man who could have died from loss of blood. He was now, according to the chart, two-hundred-nineteen pounds of restless sea lion.

"I want out of here. Every minute I stay in this white tomb I'm losing money."

"Your arm—"

"Fix it so I can at least get back to the boat, direct the boys where to go, lend my good arm to pulling up the nets when the shrimping is hot."

"Relax, Captain. Lay back. Let me take a look at how you're healing, and then we'll discuss your options."

Mac slammed his head back on the pillow wincing from the sudden movement. *The woman said options. Play along, stupid. She's the only one who can help you get out of this straight jacket. If she doesn't play ball with you, then … then you'll walk out.* Mac smiled. The man who had to be in control had just come up with a plan of action … walk out, walk away from the nurses' peering eyes, the infernal clicking of heels down the hallway, and the constant blood pressure wrap on his good arm, thermometers, and skimpy meals. Hell, he could waste away in here if he stayed much longer.

Maria squinted at Mac's face as she removed the bandages from his upper arm extending to his shoulder. Her patient had settled back too quickly. She'd bet anything he had a scheme on how he was going to escape his confinement. She had saved him for the end of her afternoon rounds. She knew it was going to be a struggle to keep him much longer. Maybe she could talk him into giving her one more day. After all it was a nasty gash that ripped through the muscle and nicked the bone. So much tissue she'd had to repair before stitching him back together.

"So, how's she look? Pretty good, huh?" Mac was holding his jaw tight refusing to give into the pain as Maria, gentle as she was, removed the dressings underneath.

Giving him a quick glance Maria set about applying fresh bandages.

Her fleeting look startled him. He had never seen eyes that color—dark violet. A white mask hung down from around her neck onto her white coat. Her hair, what he could see was reddish brown, pulled back tight from her face into a, what did women call that? Oh yeah, a French twist. He chuckled, thinking that another man, Studs for instance, would have made a play for the pretty doctor with the violet eyes. Well, he'd leave Miss Violet eyes to him. He didn't care what color her eyes were, he wanted out of her constant pawing at his arm. The woman just couldn't seem to let well enough alone. She had his arm thumping worse than ever.

Hearing the chuckle, Maria raised her eyes from securing the last piece of tape. "What's so funny, Mac?"

Smiling, Mac glanced down at her left hand. No ring. Maybe she didn't wear a ring when she was playing doctor. "You married?"

Maria's eyes widened. That was the last question she thought would come from Mac's mouth. Many male patients had tried to hustle her but none like this one.

"No, Captain Macintyre. Not now, not ever." Her words emphatic as she slipped the white compression sleeve over his arm.

Whoa, she's been hurt by some guy with that angry retort.

Boisterous laughter preceded Mac's crew as Studs, Shrimp, and Sissy filled the hospital room with playful clowning. They quickly stifled their antics and stood at attention, red ball caps in hand, the picture of proper decorum staring at their skipper. That is Shrimp and Sissy looked at Mac. Studs was taking in Dr. Grayson from stem to stern, pausing at the stern, then back up to her eyes.

"Captain, we had a good day—over a hundred pounds of red snapper, the most beautiful bad boys you'd ever hope to see," Sissy chortled. "We even cleaned up, showered, this time … in your honor. See, clean T-shirts and shorts." Three faces beamed at their skipper with Star Fish Market printed in white on their black shirts, toes hugging flip-flops of various colors.

Maria's lips drew up thinking how lucky Mac was to have such a crew. She picked up his chart from the bedside table updating the change in dressing and her observations of how he was healing.

"Nasty oil rig fire due south of New Orleans," Sissy said twisting his cap with his fingers.

"Any oil spilled?" Mac asked.

"Naw." Shrimp said towering above his two buddies. "Just trying to see if I could get a rise out of you. Came right back at me. Can we take him outta here, Doc? Seems his old surly self," Shrimp asked, his white teeth brilliant against his black skin.

"Not tonight. Not tomorrow. After that we'll see. You're from New Orleans, Mac?"

"Mom was born there—"

"Who's born where?" Regina said as she strode into the room giving Mac a kiss on the forehead. "Oh, you three. Leaving? So I can talk to my son? How are you, dear? Resting I hope, although …" Regina shot a dismissive eye at the three disheveled seamen and then looked at the doctor who was staring strangely back at her.

"Regina, be nice," Mac said. "These guys are keeping your namesake afloat, and, from the sounds of it, keeping themselves and me in more than beer money."

"Bye, Mac. We'll come by tomorrow—check on your progress. See what time we can pick you up," Studs said raking his fingers through his sandy waves with a wink at Maria.

"Hey, I didn't say he would be discharged," Maria said muscling in front of Sissy to replace the chart on the end of the bed.

"We're leaving. We're leaving. Nice to see you Mrs. Macintyre." Sissy said, a colorful kerchief tied in back holding his inky black hair.

Chattering, the crew stumbled out of the room elbowing each other, Studs mumbling something about the pretty doc.

"I'll stop by in the morning, Captain. Have a restful night," Maria said smiling at Mac and nodding to his mother.

Leaving mother and son, Maria's brain was spinning with puzzle pieces. Putting the names together, Regina and Macintyre and New Orleans, she wondered if it was possible Regina Macintyre was *the* Regina Parsons that Marianne Grayson, Maria's mother, had told her daughter about? *The* Regina who stepped in and married her sister's fiancé when Patty Sue Parsons ran away from her groom on their wedding day? Marianne had said she was to be Patty Sue's bridesmaid.

The Regina Macintyre she saw next to Mac's bed definitely came from money. The hard years as a fisherman's wife had not dulled her sense of style or the manner in which she carried herself. Her light-blue silk dress was not purchased at a bargain basement, and her blond hair was perfectly cut to soften the angles of her face. Regina Macintyre was an aristocrat, a Parsons in every sense of the word. *Mummy and Daddy must be slipping her money ... if they're still living. I'll have to ask Mac about his parents. Of course, it's none of my business. But ...*

Maria stopped at the nurses' station to look up her patient's records on the computer. The screen displayed Mac's mother and father as the people to contact—Daniel and Regina Macintyre.

Chapter 11

Anna Maria Island

A soft westerly breeze flowed over Anna Maria Island and the mainland city of Bradenton. Maria swiped at a wisp of hair in her eyes anchoring it behind her ear. Her mind was bouncing between names of people she had heard in the past but now seemed to be coalescing around her patient, Charles Daniel Macintyre. Looking down at the pavement she passed her car in the hospital parking lot. Bewildered by the street that stretched in front of her, she pivoted, retracing her steps to find her car.

Driving over the Manatee Bridge onto the island she decided that after changing into shorts and a tank top at the beach house she was tending for a fellow surgeon and his wife, she'd call her mom to see if she could help fit the names together as they related to each other. She was well aware that coincidences do happen, but who would have thought that she would be the attending surgeon for a man with a tie to her own mother in New Orleans.

Fifteen minutes later, with her cell in one hand and a glass of wine in the other, she curled up on a swing overlooking the Gulf waters, and called her mom.

"Sunrise House."

"Hi, this is Maria Grayson. Can you take a phone to my mother, Marianne Grayson?"

Maria took a sip of wine wondering if her mother was having a good day or a bad day. Alzheimer's was taking a toll on her. If it was good she might remember something of the past. A bad day ... the conversation would be brief.

"Hello. Maria?" Marianne Grayson said with a lilt

Ah a good sign. "Hi, Mom. How are you feeling today?"

"I'm fine. The sun is out. Where are you?"

"I just left the hospital, finished rounds a tad early and headed to the island to cool off, and I'm now having a glass of wine talking to you."

"That's nice, dear."

Taking a deep breath, Maria plunged ahead hoping to jog her mother's memory. "Mom, you once mentioned the name of Regina Macintyre. Tell me about her or, more to the point, about her family. Do you remember her?"

"Oh, that's out of the past. What happened? Did she come in for a heart operation? Her heart could use some tweaking as I recall. Haven't seen her for ages. Not since she and Danny left New Orleans ... my dear Danny. They followed their son ... no that's not right ... she and her son ... no ... to some kind of ... an island I believe. Why?"

"Well, the son you mentioned, *Charles Macintyre, don't-call-me-Charles, call me Mac,*" Maria chuckled, "came in with a mangled arm from a fishing accident. I wouldn't have given the name a second thought but three of his crazy, *I mean certifiable crazy,* crew members came into his room and said something about New Orleans. Then this woman strides into his room like she's the chief benefactor for the hospital. She turns out to be his mother, and Mac calls her Regina. Do you think the Regina you knew and this Regina are one in the same?"

"Well, fishing, a Macintyre, and a woman named Regina tells me she could be ... maybe."

"Yeah, I saw Regina and Daniel Macintyre listed as his mother and father, emergency contacts, on Mac's hospital record."

"Snoopy little girl aren't you."

"Hey, he's my patient ... I should find out all I can about him ... in order to help with his recovery."

"Oh sure. If he looks anything like his father he must be very handsome. Married? Was that in his records?"

"Yes, he's good looking, and no, he's not married. At least there wasn't a notation he had a wife."

"And did he inquire if you were married?" her mom asked.

Wow, this wonderful. A real conversation. She's having a very good day. Only lost her train of thought once. "Yes, he did ask me."

"My, my, a little doctor-patient romance should speed up his recovery unless he decides it's more romantic to stay in bed."

"Mother, really."

"I have a picture somewhere ... there it is on my dresser. I'll send it to you."

"By the way, dear, a man called today asking for you ... I think it was today ... could have been last week."

"Who, Mom?"

"I don't know. Didn't leave his name ... or did he? I think he hung up before I had a chance to ask. I told him you worked at a hospital, and he asked the name of the hospital. I said ... don't know what I said ... oh, I think I said Florida Memorial, and poof he was gone. I never got a chance to say where it was ... suppose he'll call back if he can't find you."

"Mom, I'm at Manatee Memorial. But you were right about Florida. Maybe a former patient ... Tulane Hospital in New Orleans before I became affiliated with Manatee. Thanks, Mom, for the info on the Macintyre's. One more thing. Do you remember Regina's family name?"

"Umm ... oh yes. Parsons. Dr. Charles and Doris Parsons."

"Mom, the picture you have on your dresser, who's in it?"

"Oh a bride ... Regina and I ...and ... another woman. The bride was modeling her wedding gown. Oh my God, that's not right. Regina was the bride, she took him away from me. Had a baby ... no, no, Patty Sue had the baby, no."

Maria pulled the phone from her ear at the crash of the phone on tile. "Mom? Mom?"

Maria heard footsteps running ... louder and louder. Then the phone disconnected. Maria placed the call again.

"Sunset House—"

"I was just talking to my mother, Marianne Grayson. Something happened. Is she all right?"

"One moment please."

Maria hopped off the swing, walked out through the French doors to the narrow deck, head down. *I pushed her too hard. Shouldn't have...*

"Hello, Dr. Grayson?"

"Yes. Is my mother okay?"

"The nurse found her curled up next to her dresser. She's very agitated but we got her back into bed. I gave her a shot and she's calmer now."

"We were having a wonderful conversation … best in weeks … but suddenly—"

"I'm sorry, Dr Grayson. But it happens. She'll be fine."

"Nurse, she mentioned a picture on her dresser."

"Yes, I see it."

"Can you make a copy? Send it to me … not the original because it obviously means a lot to her."

"Of course. I'll see that you get a copy. There are names on the back: Regina, Doris, Patty Sue, Marianne."

Maria hung up the phone, padded on her bare feet into the kitchen to refill her wine glass. *Interesting,* she thought. *Mom gave me information but it seemed to be garbled ... more puzzle pieces to put together. And ... I wonder why Mac didn't want to be called Charles. Dr. Parsons would be his maternal grandfather. And a picture. Wonder if I'll recognize Regina ... she's much older now.*

The conversation with her mother had been better than she hoped for but something Marianne said hit a nerve. *A man had called looking for her.*

Chapter 12

*Hard Rock Casino,
Tampa*

Danny Macintyre left his son's hospital room as evening was falling over the west coast of Florida. He climbed into his beat-up truck and headed east on Manatee Avenue to Route 75 north to Tampa. He had joined the crew on The Regina, taking up the slack while his son was laid up, and the boys had a great day shrimping. Five-hundred dollars was burning a hole in his pocket. He knew tonight was the night he was going to hit it big. The tables were calling to him.

Turning off the highway, he promptly rolled onto North Orient Road and then there she was—Hard Rock Casino. The white 190,000 square foot, twelve-story building was bathed in soft pale purple and blue lights under a blanket of stars.

Danny's pulse quickened as he parked next to a black Mercedes. Jumping out of his truck, he gazed at the black car. She was a beauty. He blew a moist breath of air on the Mercedes' side-view mirror and rubbed the sleeve of his shirt against the glass removing the imaginary spot. Oh, yes, it was going to be a good night.

Entering the casino he strolled by the guitars mounted along the walls—the initial display of the casino's rock-and-roll theme. He smiled as the music of the slots greeted him flashing their cherries, oranges, and JACKPOT graphics. He plucked a dollar from the wad of bills in his pocket and pushed the button of the nearest dollar slot. The bad girl flashed her neon lights framing her body, round and round the rows sped by, settling down to a gush of tokens cascading into the tray.

"Holy crap. Fifty bucks. Lady luck you are with me tonight. Is that you, Patty Sue? Are you looking out for your Danny boy? Well, come on, sugar, let's head for the tables." Grinning, he scooped up the tokens, stuffed them in the right-leg pocket of his cargo pants, smacked the strips of nylon shut tight and continued on the carpeted path to the tables, the musical fruit caressing his ear drums as he left the slots behind.

"Let's warm up with a few hands of Pai Gow. Whatta ya say, Patty Sue? A nice sociable game—play against the dealer. No worrying about what the other guys and dolls are holding, and Patty Sue, you gotta love those wild jokers."

Danny stopped at the teller window and asked for a stack of dollar chips along with several five-dollar and ten-dollar chips. Handing the attendant five one-hundred dollar bills he received a tray holding his chips in return. He hiked up on a chair at a table with a little sign indicating Pai Gow was the game being played here. Players anteed up a chip to start the play, and the dealer flipped a card off the top of the deck laying it in front of the players until each player had seven cards including himself. The dealing complete, the players separated their cards into two hands: a hand of two cards and a hand of five. To win each hand had to be higher than the dealer's two hands. If one hand was higher but not the second it was considered a tie—no money changes hands.

Danny was hot. No ties for him.

Tripling his money, Danny slid off the chair, said goodbye to the other players who were relieved to see him go, hoping the guy would leave lady luck at their table.

Danny moved on to seven-card stud. This was his game. He also liked Texas Hold'em. Here you played against the other players not the dealer. Danny preferred this game, thought it took more skill. He had to read his competition, watch their body language while not giving anything away through his own facial expressions.

He had spotted four novice players, two couples on vacation joking around. Grinning, he sat down at their table. Oh yeah, he knew how to keep a poker face. Sure enough he doubled his money quickly.

A man, black Stetson pulled down on his forehead, joined the table sliding onto a chair across from Danny, resting his alligator cowboy boots on the rungs. A white shirt was tucked into jeans held by a wide black leather belt anchored with a massive silver buckle featuring a fancy crest of some kind. His shirt, open several buttons, revealed a jade pendant hanging from a bolo tie.

Danny immediately noticed the man's glass eye. Sizing up the enemy was a canny trait he possessed, one that had certainly helped him so far tonight.

The dealer nodded to the man. "Nice to see you, Wiley."

Wiley returned the nod. Because of his glass eye you couldn't' be sure where he was looking, threw players off, but not Danny.

The game proceeded with the new player. Banter between the players ceased—the game had turned serious.

Hand after hand was dealt, Danny winning most of them. He knew Wiley was testing him, but Danny had parlayed his initial stake that he walked into the casino with to almost eight-thousand dollars.

The dealer dealt the first card of a new hand. At each card the players added chips to the pot, only one throwing in his hand. Danny couldn't believe his cards. He let the pot build, Wiley matching him chip for chip. Then it was time to pounce. Danny, feeling in a trance as his hands pushed his chips to the center of the green felt, went all in. His four kings prevailed. He won the pot. Scraping the pile of chips to him, he stacked them neatly in his tray. A cool nineteen grand!

"Excuse me, folks, I think I better stop while I'm ahead. Hope you have a nice vacation," he said smiling at the couples and nodding to the black Stetson.

Wiley leaned back as Danny left the table and then excused himself, following the big winner to the parking garage.

"Hey," Wiley called out.

Danny turned. His neck hairs prickled, nerves sparking. He didn't say anything as Wiley sauntered up to him and leaned against the Mercedes.

"How about we play again. Give me chance to even the score," Wiley drawled.

"No *score* to even. I had a good night," Danny said climbing into the cab of his truck, nerves relaxing.

"Well, that's right. I could learn from you … tomorrow night?"

"Can't, but maybe sometime in the next few days," Danny said turning the key in the ignition.

"I look forward to it. I'm here most nights. Just ask for me. Ask if Wiley is playing tonight. They'll find me."

"Okay, Wiley. Bye."

Maybe I will, Danny thought. *Wiley. Stands for what? Wiley-one or sucker? I can play with a few hundred bucks. If he's a sucker I keep playing. If Wiley means Slicker and I lose, then it's hasta la vista, Mr. Wiley.*

Chapter 13

Manatee Memorial Hospital, Bradenton

6 a.m. Breakfast carts clattered down the hallway of the orthopedic floor. Nurses chattered in hushed whispers, giggling as they swapped tales of their escapades the night before.

Noise. People noise. Racket. Not the lapping of waves against the hull of a boat. Mac cursed. Wished he was on The Regina stowing the bait, the ice, pulling away from the dock with the other commercial fishermen. Three days he'd been confined to the hospital bed. According to Gail, his intern, he was progressing nicely. Moving from the ICU to the orthopedic floor was definitely a step in the right direction but not big enough, not out the front door.

Tugging at his pillow, scrunching up on the elbow of his good arm, Mac leaned back as Gail came through the door wearing a big grin over a joke heard in the hall as well as the sight of her patient's scowl.

"Good morning, Captain. I see you're in a good mood today, and wait until you see the breakfast I ordered special for you." She cranked up his bed, pushed the table covering the bedding up to his chest being mindful of his arm. Walking around the table she popped the stainless steel cover off his breakfast plate. "Lookie. Sausage and scrambled eggs, two pieces of whole wheat toast, and … a side of blueberry pancakes and a carafe holding two cups of black coffee."

She beamed into his face waiting for his reaction glancing away only to fill his coffee mug.

She didn't have to wait long.

"You're an angel, Gail. This is what I call a breakfast. When doc comes in I'm going to be stoked and ready to roar out of here," Mac said picking up his fork and stabbing a large bite of sausage.

"You're welcome. Would you like a repeat tomorrow morning?"

"No. I'll be long gone. Plan to be pulling away from the dock at this time tomorrow."

"Whoa there, mister," Dr. Grayson admonished as she strolled in taking his chart from Gail's outstretched hand.

Mac chuckled. He was ready. He intended to try a new approach on the good doctor—honey instead of vinegar. She seemed to be in a good mood—fresh green scrubs under her white coat adorned with a stethoscope necklace. Yup, she was a vision with a smile. He was going to play her like a red snapper snared by a hook at the end of his line.

"How's the pain?" Maria asked as he pushed a forkful of blueberry pancake slathered with butter and syrup into his mouth.

"Dang. Would you look at that? I need a bib. Big old blueberry got away from me and stained my pretty flowered gown." Chuckling, he pulled the garment a trifle to show her the stain. Gail giggled and left the doctor with her patient.

"I asked about your pain, Captain."

"Practically gone. Those big bad boys are doing the trick."

"Pain tablets?"

"Whatever. I feel like a new man with this breakfast. How about having a cup of coffee with me? Extra cup right here."

"Can't. Surgery this morning. But ask for an extra cup this afternoon with your lunch tray and I'll take you up on that offer." Maria read the morning lab report Gail had entered on the chart. "I see your hemoglobin count is a 9—"

"Ah, and a big old 9 means I can be released."

"And you found that out how?"

"Hey, a guy doesn't divulge all his secrets, at least not while the damsel has the upper hand—tray table blocking my escape not to mention my arm that manages to shoot streaks of pain through those stitches you so kindly gave me. Then there's this very unflattering flowered thing I'm wearing ... kinda wearing. Very fashionable—just above the knee. Would be easier if the thing opened in the front so I could pee—"

"Okay, Mac. I get the picture. See you at lunch. Now," she paused, a frown spreading along her lips. "When do you expect the three pirates?"

"Sissy called. Should be here about four o'clock. Why?"

"Big day. I asked them to come by. They're going to learn how to change your dressing. Depending on how that goes, I may … *may* … release you tomorrow morning."

"Yes, ma'am. I'll be sure they're here. Four o'clock. Now, if you'll just move this table, I have to go wrestle with this gown thing in the bathroom."

"Bye, Mac. See you later," she said guiding the tray table to clear his arm. "I have a date with a gall bladder." She laughed at his grimace while hanging the chart on the bed and walked swiftly from the room leaving him to wrestle with the flowered thing.

Maria stood to the side of the nurse's station, leaning against the counter updating the charts of her surgery patients, when a man in a black suit and tie, graying at the temples, approached.

"Excuse me, Dr. Grayson, my name is Ross Bennett. Is there someplace we can talk, my dear?"

Maria looked up in surprise. "How do you know I'm Dr. Grayson? Who are you? Insurance—"

"No, ma'am. Not insurance. A lawyer. As to how I know you're Dr. Grayson, you fit the description I was given."

"Good heavens, Mr. Bennett, is one of my patients wanted—"

"No, no. Not one of your patients. I'm investigating a case, something that happened two years ago … when you were a resident in New Orleans."

Maria's heart spiked, stomach twisted. However, her face showed none of her internal reactions. "I can't imagine how I can help. There's a visitor's waiting area at the end of the hall. We can talk there."

Walking side by side they stepped back at the sound of fast moving footsteps, muffled on the linoleum floor. Orderlies pushing a patient's bed shot by.

"I suppose you have some sort of identification?" Maria asked. She glanced at the suit then nodded to the empty chairs lined up against the white walls and a magazine-strewn table off to the side.

"Yes, of course," Bennett said setting his briefcase next to the chair as he sat down. "Here's my card."

As Bennett dug out a business card from his wallet a man rounded the corner, bumped into a chair dropping his newspaper. Both Bennett and Dr. Grayson looked up as the man squatted, picked up his paper, mumbled something about being clumsy and continued down the hall to the elevator.

Maria looked at the card the lawyer handed to her. "Well, I suppose anybody could have a business card printed but I'll take you at your word," she replied pocketing the card. "Now what's this case?"

"I've been retained by a surgeon at Tulane Hospital to look into the death of a Mr. Arturo Perez. You were just completing your residency ... as a surgeon ... general surgery, no specialty or at least not at that time. Have you begun training for a specialty, Doctor? Cardiac?"

"No. The patients arriving in critical condition in the ER are my *specialty* for now, if you want to call it a specialty." Maria concentrated on her breathing—controlled—in, out.

"I see. Well Mr. Perez was a patient undergoing heart surgery ... two years ago. His surgeon asked some questions because he did not believe that Mr. Perez died as reported. Unsatisfied with the answers he received, he contacted me to look into the matter."

Maria looked into Bennett's eyes with a blank stare. "Mr. Bennett, I was a resident at the Tulane Medical Center that year, but I don't know of a Perez, and I would not have been part of Mr. Perez's surgical team to repair his heart." Maria stood. As far as she was concerned, this conversation was over. "So, as I said, I can't help you."

Bennett stood, pushing his tie under his suit jacket, facing Maria. "Dr. Grayson, I'm not here to ask about your participation in his surgery. I'm here because in my research you were on the list as being on duty the day Arturo Perez died ... on the ICU floor ... after his surgery. Dr. Grayson, I'm here to ask you if you saw anything unusual that day, March twenty-third, on that floor, ICU, bed one?"

"Mr. Bennett, I can assure you I saw nothing irregular, nothing that would obviously cause the death of a patient. Now, if you have no further questions, I'm scheduled in the OR in five minutes and I have to scrub. Good luck with your case."

Maria turned, strode down the hall disappearing around the corner to scrub for the removal of a gall bladder. Entering the scrub room she tied the green scrub cap over her hair, tied the white mask over her nose and mouth, and squirted antibacterial soap on her hands and forearms rubbing her skin under the water streaming from the faucet, all the while concentrating on her breathing. Her breathing under control, she walked into the blazing lights of the operating room.

Chapter 14

A beat-up green Ford coupe idled at the end of a row of cars in the Manatee Memorial Hospital parking lot bordered by expansive lawns. The driver, a little man, scrunched down behind the wheel, his New Orleans Saints ball cap shadowing a smile as he selected the code from his cell's directory.

"Junior?"

"Who do you think it is, stupid?"

"Just making sure. I have good news."

"Give it to me, Wally. I don't have all day."

"The woman, you know, the one—"

"I know, I know. Did you find her?"

"Dr. Grayson is a surgeon at a hospital, Bradenton, Florida. And, she knows nothing."

"You sound sure of yourself."

"It was beautiful, Junior. Actually, I think you should give me a bonus because—"

"Wally!"

"Okay, okay. I lucked out. I had no more than walked into the hospital than this guy brushes past me. Honest to God, Junior, my karma was red hot, like I willed it."

"So, who was he?"

"A lawyer I've been tailing, the lawyer for the surgeon at the New Orleans hospital, you know, who I alerted you to the last time we talked. I tracked him—no more than thirty minutes ago—to a nurse's station where he walks up to this woman, introduces himself and says he wants to talk to her. Eureka! He and I were looking for the same dame. All my assignments should be so easy," Wally snickered taking a deep breath, waiting for a reaction from his boss.

"So?"

"He said something. She said something. They started walking down the hall. I watched, waited to see where they go. Bided my time … can't rush this undercover stuff."

"Wally, stop patting yourself on the back. What then?"

"Shear brilliance that's what. They sat down, like at a visitor's area. I hustled passed them, dropped my newspaper … when I'm undercover I always carry a newspaper just in case. When I bent over to pick it up I smacked a bug under the chair a few feet from them and then went on my merry way."

"That is good. What did they say?"

"I heard everything. Naturally not what they said before they sat down but after. The conversation was definitely about Perez. Bennett, that's the lawyer, tells the lady doctor that Perez's surgeon was skeptical about his death. Thinks he didn't die from his surgery. Bennett said the doc, the Grayson dame, was on duty that day. Asked her if she saw anything strange going on in Perez's room. Grayson said … swore she saw nothing unusual and was not involved in Perez's surgery. Period. End of story."

Wally waited for his boss to congratulate him but Junior wasn't talking.

"Junior, you there?" Was the line dead? Wally looked at the display on his phone. Maybe there'd been a satellite interruption.

"Junior?"

"Now you listen to me, Wally. Maybe she was telling the truth and maybe she wasn't. I want you to tail her. Maybe that lawyer spooked her. I'm not satisfied."

"Well, you should be satisfied. You're in the clear. I'll send you a copy of what they said so you can hear it for yourself."

"Do that. And, Wally, I want a tight tail on this woman for at least two weeks just in case. I want to know where she goes, who she meets, talks to."

"Patients too?"

Wally waited. Looked at his phone. The line was dead.

Chapter 15

Mac jerked his legs out from under the sheet and was rewarded with a shock of pain in his upper arm for his impatience. He had to get out of the hospital, away from Dr. Grayson and the insane thoughts that had crept into his mind, taking over his mind of seeing her outside, outside in something other than the infernal scrubs she wore.

"You're crazy, Macintyre," he muttered as he got to his feet. "That's it, no more dizzies ... dang hemoglobb thing must be a 10." *See her outside? No way. Get yourself back to The Regina, back to the sea.* He walked gingerly to the window testing his strength, turned back to the bed catching a glimpse of his face in the bathroom mirror. He looked like a grizzly bear. He bypassed the bed choosing to sit in the chair instead. He'd show her. He was ready to leave her prying eyes, her violet eyes.

Would this day ever end, he wondered, sweeping a lock of thick, black hair from his eyes. He decided the chair was uncomfortable went back to the bed, stretched out, shut his eyes, shut out violet eyes.

"Hey, Mac, we're here. Crew to Captain. Knock, knock. Are you there?" Sissy whispered in Mac's ear.

Thoughts of Maria lingered in his mind, her eyes warm, her lips touching his. He swatted at his ear tickled by Sissy's warm breath. Opened his eyes. "What the ... Sissy, what're you doing?"

"Getting your attention," Studs laughed. "Where were you anyway?"

"Right here in this bed and don't think I can't whip all of you if you do something silly. I have four units of super-hero blood in me don't forget," Mac shot back at his crew as Maria entered the room. He caught her quick glance, something in her eyes he hadn't seen before. Concern? No, more like fear. Something was wrong. She didn't smile, no hello, no joking with the guys. She was all business.

Checking his chart, she looked up at the three crewmen arrayed in front of her. "I see everyone is ready to practice changing Mac's dressing. Please stand at the end of the bed. I'll go through the procedure first, and then it'll be your turn to change the bandages covering the incision. Mac, who's staying with you for the next couple of days? I—"

"I don't need a babysitter, Doc. No one is going to be staying with me."

"You've just been through a traumatic ordeal—"

"Yeah, real traumatic with this doctor here," Shrimp interjected giving his eyebrows two quick pumps.

"Must have been *awful*," Studs chimed in chuckling.

"Push a little red button and nurses rush to your side," Sissy added sending the three of them into fits of laughter, tears rolling down their cheeks. "I'd sure like to be in that there bed tended by Doc Grayson." Sissy could barely talk he was laughing so hard.

"Okay, fellas, let's get this done. I have other patients to see."

Her curt reply brought the three to attention swallowing their laughter, wiping away their tears with the back of their hands.

Maria rolled the tray table to Mac's chest resting his arm on top and then lined up several pairs of white latex gloves, a pile of 4-by-4 inch gauze pads, a role of tape, a pair of scissors, and a fresh compression sleeve.

"First, wash up at the bathroom sink. There's antiseptic soap in the pump bottle. Then come back and put on a pair of these gloves. I picked up the largest ones I could find. Go ahead. Scoot," she said. Her tone was sharp. "Dry your hands good and then come back and pull the gloves on. It's important you wear fresh gloves every time for the next several days when you check Mac's arm to be sure the wound remains clean. I'm sure the captain would not want to come back here because one of you gives him an infection."

"You've got that right," Mac said, watching Maria. Something was definitely wrong but he couldn't inquire with these three clowns around ready to convulse into laughter and, oh yeah, he knew the hilarity was going to erupt again. The only way his three new nurses could handle this situation was by laughing. He knew they were not going to like what they saw under the bandage. A quick smile flicked over his lips at the thought of Studs fainting, although, maybe he was wrong. They had, after all, saved his life.

Maria nodded at the men to get with it ... pull on the gloves. Her brows up, she waved a pair under Sissy's nose.

"Studs, you go first. If you can get the gloves over those knurly knuckles of yours then I guess Shrimp and I can," Sissy said chuckling accompanied by a snicker from Shrimp.

Studs stepped forward, nodded to the doctor, raised his brows back at her and daintily plucked a glove from her fingers. He looked at Mac then his two comrades. "Just watch, you guys. I'll show you how it's done." He stuck his fist into the glove, then opened his fingers, tried to extend his fingers.

"Oh, yeah, that's how it's done, all right," Shrimp said. "Stick your fingers out first, you knucklehead."

Studs tried again, playing to his audience and with great difficulty pulled the latex over his huge fingers. He finally had both gloves on holding his hands in the air triumphantly. "There, see, just like the doc here," he said smugly. "Now you two smarty pants try it."

Mimicking Studs, Shrimp and Sissy were quick and waiting for the next step. All three stood at the end of the bed, elbows bent holding up their latex-gloved hands in the air smiling like catfish set to snatch a minnow.

"Ready when you are, Doc," Shrimp said.

Mac noticed that his guys brought a quick smile to Maria's beautiful lips, which to his consternation brought back his dream of those lips on his.

"Next you'll remove the dressing. The wound is about five inches long to just above the elbow," Maria said pointing along the top of his arm. "Don't touch the wound if you can help it."

"Yeah, or you'll get a fist in the nose with my good hand," Mac said screwing his face to a mean scowl.

Maria ignored his threat and began her demonstration removing everything covering the incision but the blood-stained gauze.

When Studs saw the blood, he moved to the end of the line. He wasn't going to be first this time.

Maria gently removed the bloody gauze. Although sticking to his skin Mac saw there was no fresh blood. His arm seemed to be healing nicely but when she dabbed at the wound with a wipe soaked with alcohol his muscle tightened in response, shooting pain through his arm. Maria didn't look up as she cleaned the dried blood. The alcohol stung the fresh wound again and Mac's bicep contracted, but he made no sound, didn't pull back, the only outward sign of pain had come from his muscle. However, his right hand balled into a tight fist under the sheet.

His control was not missed by the doctor. She saw his muscle react and fist balling under the cover. She returned the layers of fresh dressing and then nodded to Shrimp to repeat what she had shown them.

Shrimp stepped up, gave a couple of fist pumps and removed the compression sleeve.

Mac winced. "Hey, Dr. Grayson said to stay away from the wound. Once more and I swear you'll have a black eye."

With the warning, Shrimp deftly removed the dressing. His fingers jerky at first then relaxed as he concentrated on what he was supposed to do.

Sissy performed the routine perfectly—again his initial movements were clumsy but then settled down. "See, that's how it's done, Studs. Pretty good, huh, Mac?"

"Yeah, you're a regular Florence Nightingale."

Studs, all business, also performed without mishap. Looking at Maria for approval, he received a smile for his efforts. "Anytime you want me to assist you just let me know, Doc."

Maria did not respond. No smile. All business. "As you saw, gentlemen, the gauze may stick to the incision from blood seepage as the wound heals. By tomorrow that should be a non-issue. Don't put the used gauze anywhere but in a plastic bag. The sleeve must be the correct size—not too tight or too loose. Its job is to secure the dressing underneath and control swelling. When you finish remove your gloves, put them in the plastic bag, and toss everything you touched into the wastebasket. Use the same sleeve unless it's blood stained. It can be washed. There will be extra in the kit of supplies I'm preparing for you when he leaves the hospital. That's it, Mac. Gail will do a final check on your hemoglobin count in the morning. If it's still nine or better I'll sign the release form."

Chapter 16

Mac pushed away the tray table. He was ready to be released, anxious to get out of his confinement, but he wasn't going to put up with any wheelchair nonsense. He would walk out the front door. But one thing was for sure, he was going to miss the special breakfasts, the extra large helping of sausage and scrambled eggs and toast that Gail managed to wheedle out of the hospital's kitchen.

Maria looked at her patient still in the johnny shirt, legs over the side of the bed. He didn't look like a tough-as-nails fisherman in that get up. But he did look like he was ready to spring off the bed, race down the hall where his buddies were waiting, and cruise out to sea on The Regina.

Yesterday the boys had passed the test. They changed the dressing with chuckles, cursing, and laughter. Nonetheless they did a good job and she had congratulated them as she handed them the duffle bag with a four-day supply of bandages. Sissy had left a change of clothes he picked up for Mac on the chair.

"I have something for you, a waterproof sleeve to cover the compression sleeve and dressing. The waterproof sheathing includes a pump that sucks the air out from under the cover, forming a tight seal against your arm. Your arm will stay dry when completely submerged underwater."

"Blue. Very fashionable. Looks like a long mitt you'd use to take something out of the oven. Thanks."

"Now you're telling me you cook?"

"Movies."

"You don't have to thank me. It's on your bill plus here's a list of pharmacies where you can buy a backup sleeve if you need it. They're not expensive."

There it was again … Maria was all business, distant, her eyes … her eyes what? Fearful? Maybe. He was going to find out. No harm in asking her out to dinner … maybe he could help. If she didn't accept his invitation then that was it. *No. Don't get involved. DON'T' get involved.*

"I've set up a schedule for rehab work on your arm—should be for six weeks. If you can manage three times a week at first, your arm will regain strength faster. The therapist will make that decision."

Gail bustled in with a bag laying it on the foot of the bed. "Your stuff … when you were admitted. Your clothes were beyond saving—bloody. But, there's a couple pieces of jewelry—your watch and a medal."

Mac put on his watch and then pulled out the Saint Christopher medal, rubbing his thumb over the gold—the medal his father's runaway bride had given to her fiancé. His pops had worn it every day for as long as Mac could remember until he gave it to Mac the day he took over as Captain of The Regina.

Maria watched him finger the medal and then she turned to leave. Mac reached for her arm, held it firmly. "Maria, have dinner with me next week. You say the night. I owe you."

"Oh, you'll get a bill all right, Captain."

"No, I owe you something that isn't on the bill. You put this humpty dumpty together again. You were patient with my crew, put up with our cussing … and … I want to see you, outside of this sterile place. Please, have dinner with me. Tell me the night, the time, and where to pick you up."

Maria hesitated. She had a rule against seeing a patient on the outside. It could be misinterpreted. But Mac was different and oh, how she wanted a friend, needed a friend to talk to. A fisherman. They were worlds apart. Nothing could come of it but friendship. But … there was always a *but*. "Friday night, next week, eight o'clock, out front of the hospital. I have consultations but should be done by then. Give me your cell number so I can call if things change."

Mac took the slip of paper and the pen she handed to him, wrote the number and handed it back to her. There. He asked her. She accepted. Why in the name of all the sea monsters in the Gulf did he do it?

"Mac, I'm here to take you home," the man's boisterous voice declared as he came through the door. He was the spitting image of Mac but much older and rather worse for wear.

"Pops, what are you doing here? The boys and I are heading out as soon as my doc here signs that paper in front of her.

"Hold on, Mac, I have something to tell you. Something big," Danny said grinning ear to ear.

"Can't it wait until tonight? You and Mom can tell me when I stop in for dinner."

"Nope. Can't wait and I don't want your mother to know ... not yet anyway. Sorry, Doc, but this is just between father and son."

"Oh, no you don't, Pops. You have something to say you can say it in front the doc. Besides we'll treat what you say as doctor-patient confidentiality under the law."

"Okay, but I don't—"

"Spill it, Pop."

"Mac, I won big two nights ago. Would have told you then, but I wanted to make some inquires, take a look at a few boats, talk to some charter companies."

"How much have you had to drink this morning? You're not making sense." Mac stood, motioned for Maria to turn around while he pulled on his jockey shorts and jeans Sissy had picked up from his home. Dressed, he tapped her on the shoulder, and she turned back.

"Why did you do that ... checking out boats?" Mac asked.

"I banked the money so I wouldn't be tempted to go back to the Hard Rock."

"Oh, you went gambling? But you said you won ... how much?"

"Close to twenty grand."

"Holy shit. Sorry, Maria. How did you do that?"

"Well, I'd say lady luck was with me, but I really think it was Patty Sue." Daniel whispered.

Maria raised her brows to the man, then to Mac. Patty Sue was the name her mother had mentioned.

"Mac, you can get out of the fishing business ... commercial fishing ... and take up being the Captain of a charter fishing boat ... or tours ... families, kids. Not so dangerous."

"Hold it, Pops. How did you win that big? You couldn't have started with more than a few hundred dollars."

"Well, I wasn't going to tell you, but the last two hands ... I tell you son, Patty Sue was with me ... went all in."

"You what?" Mac snapped. "Did you even stop to think about the repairs we could make on The Regina with twenty grand?"

Danny stood his ground, grinning. "If I won big last night, I can win big again, Charlie boy."

That did it. The name he hated—Charles, especially Charlie. Grabbing his shirt, he tapped the bottom line of the form on the clipboard. Maria signed the form, handed it to him, and Mac stomped out but not before calling over his shoulder to Maria that he would see her next Friday at eight o'clock sharp.

Gail ran down the hall pushing the wheelchair after him screeching something about hospital rules as the fisherman managed to evade her, waving to his nurses to follow him, as he bolted out into the sunshine.

Chapter 17

Anna Maria Island

Mac had waited for this night, this time with Maria away from her work. He gazed at the beautiful woman sitting next to him, glimmers of red highlighting her dark brown hair. He had wondered what she would be like without the trappings of the hospital, her domain. Well, he found out. She looked vulnerable, soft, very female, everything he would want in a woman. And, that set off alarm bells in Mac's head: *look but don't touch. Women are trouble. The woman Pops loved most in the whole world left him, left him broken ... drinking and gambling. His mother was overprotective, a woman impossible to live with.*

The evening star shown bright in the deepening sky as the sun dipped below the horizon melting the golden waves of the Gulf to amber then dark blue. Protected inside a hurricane shade, the candle flickered in the soft breeze off the water.

Mac touched the lip of his martini glass to Maria's. "Cheers. Thanks for putting up with me and my crew," he said smiling.

"You're welcome," Maria replied, her white halter-dress taking on a soft glow in the candlelight. "How's your arm? Any pain?"

"Only when I bump it, which happens all too often. Darn thing seems to find everything within a couple of feet. I had to shop for shirts that button down the front. Can't manage to bend my arm enough to get through the armholes in my T-shirts."

"And the smoking? I notice you haven't fired one up."

"Struggling, but okay so far. Have to admit I've substituted cigars—just one, end of the day." Mac was having trouble keeping his eyes from wandering over Maria's delicate figure, the silk fabric of the dress leaving little to his imagination. The scrubs had hidden all this and now he desired more of her.

Maria's eyes took in the fisherman. He looked different—white short-sleeve shirt tucked into black trousers, his calloused feet clad in black shoes. She was familiar with the facial shadow and the touch of his arm but now the muscles exuded strength, strength she could lean on. "Your father make any more killings at the casino?"

Mac shook his head. "Not that I know of and I'm sure he'd tell me. I checked the title to The Regina. It's in my name and my name only, but he definitely got my attention. Sorry you had to hear my yelling at him. But, if Pops sold The Regina for gambling money, if I lost The Regina … well that would be the end of me."

"I doubt that, Captain. I can tell fishing is in your blood … and your feet."

"What's the matter with my feet?"

"Calloused. Brown from wearing the heavy rubber boots when you're out at sea. I've seen feet like yours a few times."

"Hmmm, other men's feet sticking out from under the covers?"

"Only *sticking out* from hospital sheets." Maria took a sip of her drink, her eyes wandering out to the waves gently lapping the beach. *Yes, strength to lean on would be different, would be wonderful.*

Mac inched his chair closer to her. They sat side by side looking at the vast sea before them. This was the first time Mac could remember that he felt relaxed when he wasn't fishing. Maria's voice was soft, gentle, resonating compassion. Practiced bedside manner, he surmised. Whatever it was he liked it. He reached for her hand holding the stem of her cocktail glass.

"You're dropping your professional doctor attitude—"

"Excuse me? Attitude?" she said softly, brows rising in mock affront but she didn't pull her hand away.

"You know what I mean. All business with the stethoscope in your ears, or eyes riveted on your watch while you count my heartbeats. Which, by the way was never accurate because when you picked up my wrist I know my heart sped up. Not fair, sweetheart," he grinned, but just thinking about her touch set his nerves to tingling.

"Oh, oh, Humphrey Bogart. Now, I'm trouble."

"Speaking of trouble, are you going to tell me what happened the other day? All of a sudden your cool professional demeanor turned to … what, I'm not sure. If I had to guess I would say to deep concern."

Maria turned away. Watched a couple walking in the surf, holding hands, shoes dangling from their fingers. Watched another beach walker, head down picking up a seashell, then ambling to an empty table, taking a seat with his back to her. He looked familiar … all beach people looked familiar.

"Ross Bennett, a lawyer, came looking for me."

"A lawyer?"

"He's working for a surgeon in New Orleans. About a dead man in a hospital where I was completing my residency."

Mac felt her hand turn cold, stiffen, but she didn't look at him so he couldn't see her eyes, what they held. Her breathing quickened.

"What did he want? Was the dead guy your patient?"

"No. Bennett wanted to talk to me, wanted to know if I remembered anything, saw anything unusual the day the man died that might help his case."

"What kind of case?"

"Not sure if it's really a case, more that the surgeon felt his patient didn't die as reported."

A waitress approached the table; Mac wagged his finger at their glasses. The waitress left to fill his order for two more drinks. "Did you see something?"

"Not really."

She started to say something more then swallowed the words, but he could tell she was remembering whatever it was in vivid color in her mind's eye.

"I told Bennett I saw nothing unusual … a man in a white coat … striped pants … bending over a patient in the bed. I thought maybe he needed assistance. He didn't."

Maria turned to Mac. He was startled at the fear in her eyes. She shuddered, drew her hand away rubbing her arm to ward off a chill.

"Maria, did you go in?"

"No, because the doctor … just then I heard my page calling me to the OR. I responded to the page. Never thought any more about it, until the end of my shift. One of the nurses commented that the man in 313 had died. He removed his IV."

"Maria, are you sure what you saw was the same patient Bennett was referring to?"

"Yes. The patient in 313. I remember because I thought 13 was an unlucky number for the patient when the nurse told me he had died."

"Do you think the doctor, the man in the coat saw you?"

"No. I don't think so. His back was to me when I paused at the door. He was turning ... I ran down the hall, rounded the corner to the scrub room answering my page. It's all silly. I saw nothing."

Mac had some knowledge of how the law worked and could understand why Maria had reason to be concerned. It had to be serious if a lawyer had tracked her down as a potential witness.

At the end of his second year of law school Mac was frustrated. He knew in his bones that law school wasn't for him. He couldn't stand being cooped up between stacks of musty leather-bound books any longer. The lure of the sea was stronger than his mother's bribes to keep him going to class. He bolted.

Shaking his head, looking at Maria's drawn face, Mac laid his hand over hers twisting the stem of her glass and changed the subject. He could circle back to the dead guy later, offer to help although he wasn't sure how. She said it was silly, really nothing, but he felt there was more. *Maybe she hadn't seen anything wrong. Now she was confused. Upset only because she had rushed away and did not offer to help. Yeah. That's it, guilty because she didn't stop to help.*

Mac sensed the tension draining from her body. She began to relax after confiding to him what she had bottled up inside. Guilt. She had suggested the cozy restaurant on the Gulf side of Holmes Beach, a mid-point on the island. The place was perfect—privacy with the melody of the waves serenading them. He leaned in and kissed her cheek lightly, squeezed her hand. He was there for her.

Mac decided to lighten the atmosphere over dinner with tales of some of his adventures with his crew, referring to them as nurses as they performed surgery cleaning the fish. Now, over coffee sitting close together in an easy silence, Mac absently felt for the gold chain around his neck. "You said you were serving your residency in New Orleans. Are you from there?" he asked.

"Yes, and you and I have a connection," she said brightly her lips drawing into a smile.

"How's that? My mom was born there—"

"I know," Maria laughed softly. "I confess. The day you became my patient, no, the day I met your mother, I talked to my mother,

Marianne Grayson. She lives in New Orleans where I was born and also grew up."

"No kidding. Should I know her?"

"No, but your father does, although he may not remember her."

Now, it was Mac's turn to raise his brows in surprise.

"My mother has Alzheimer's so her memory can be sketchy, but she knows your mother, Regina Parsons Macintyre."

Mac's eyes widened raising his brows further. "I'm so sorry about her illness ... but maybe she's mistaken ... about knowing Regina?"

"Nope. My mom was a bridesmaid for Patty Sue Parsons."

"Pop's runaway bride? She gave him this St. Christopher medal. Remember you returned it to me when you cut me loose from the hospital." Mac pulled the chain from under his open shirt displaying the medal. It was warm to his touch. "As I said before, Pops gave it to me when I took over The Regina. And now, here we are, the two of us, together on Anna Maria Island."

"Coincidences do happen you know," Maria said, her violet eyes twinkling.

"Or, sweetheart, it may be fate." Bogart picked up the lady's hand kissing her smooth warm skin.

"Hello, Junior?"

"Wally, it's about time you called. Anything new? What's she doing?"

"You may be in trouble, then again maybe not. The doc did see something but was called away at the same time. It's more like she feels bad after hearing that Perez died and that she didn't do anything to help. What do you want me to do?"

"Stay on it. Watch her for awhile longer. Let's be sure she sticks to her story."

Chapter 18

The setting sun blinded Maria as she stared out at the Gulf through the open French doors, tapping her foot on the mosaic tile in front of the swing, ruminating over the dinner with Mac. Confiding in him had been cathartic. *Cathartic? You're kidding yourself.* Her fingers traced her cheek … feeling his kiss, a kiss she wanted. *He was being kind, like a brother. You're fooling yourself, Maria. Mac may have kissed you as a brother but you didn't receive it from a brother. Admit it, your stomach twisted, breathing stopped ... only a moment ...you wanted more.*

"What difference does it make?" she mumbled shaking her head. "Worlds apart. See him again? Not likely. Why not? Oh, yes, it was more than cathartic."

I felt safe, protected for the first time since the lawyer had reignited the memory of the man in striped pants. Do I have something to fear? Or, is my imagination playing tricks? Maybe I should talk to Bennett. Find out what he thinks happened that day.

Her finger traced the gold cross hanging from a thin gold chain around her neck. Her mother had given her the family heirloom as a wedding present. Her marriage didn't last, just kids in med-school—marriage of convenience, sharing expenses—but the cross was a piece of her heritage, a piece she had precious little of. She thought of the small ruby in the center as her family's bloodline.

With a deep sigh, she walked to the dining room table, picked up Ross Bennett's business card and taped his number on her cell.

Waiting to see if he answered, hoping that he wouldn't, she kicked off her shoes and ambled back to the swing curling up against the flowered throw pillows.

"Hello, Dr. Grayson. How are you, my dear?"

"Fine, thank you. Mr. Bennett … ah, I've changed my mind. Perhaps we should re-run our last conversation. I'd like to hear—"

"I see, but not now, not over the phone. How about tomorrow, Doctor? I can be there by one o'clock. Does that work with your schedule?"

"Yes, unless there's a shooting on the beach flooding the ER with emergency surgeries."

"A bit cynical, my dear, but I understand. At the hospital?"

"Yes, the chapel. It will be private there. Ask the woman at the information desk for directions. One o'clock."

"My dear, I think it best that you not talk about my coming to see you. And, please don't tell anyone what we are going to discuss. If anyone asks, just say I'm an old friend who dropped by. After we talk, I'll advise you further. I don't want to put you in danger."

Chapter 19

The black SUV sped west on I-4 the needle firmly planted on the seventy-miles-per-hour hash mark. Manny gripped the wheel with his left hand while holding Liz's hand tightly with his right. Liz raised his knuckles to her lips, then swung her short red ponytail against Manny's shoulder to see Aunt Jane in the backseat. Jane's lips were curved, happily gazing down at the purple-flowered muumuu that covered her ample figure. Her feet up she admired her purple toes poking out through flip-flops. Her silvery-pink hair rested against a pillow. It was to be another beautiful day in paradise on Anna Maria Island.

Behind Jane in the cargo area, GumDrop was sleeping on her back in her carrier, paws in the air. Maggie and Peaches were left with Liz's mom and dad in Port Orange.

Liz kissed Manny on the cheek then leaned back against the headrest. She smiled thinking that she and her husband-to be-would never shake their investigator personas. They both were wearing white shirts tucked into black trousers, but her suitcase was crammed full with her signature outfits—capris, tops, dresses in mixtures of bold colors.

"How's that orange tiger doing?" Manny called to Jane his eyes peeled on the road but wandered every now and then to the light of his life—the sparkling redhead squeezing his hand.

"GumDrop's fine but your dogs may never speak to you guys again," Jane chuckled.

"Manny, maybe we'll have to leave Peaches and Maggie home when we get married," Liz said her big brown eyes looking up at him.

"What? No way. Peaches wants to be the ring bearer."

"And Maggie can hold my train up off the sand … not."

"You're going to have a train?"

"I'm not telling. The bride keeps her gown a secret."

"I like that word—bride," Manny said kissing the top of her hand.

"Hey, you two lovebirds, keep your eyes on the road," Jane said with a snicker. "Are we there yet?"

"Onto I-75, then thirty minutes and we'll be near the bridge to the island. How are you doing back there?" Manny asked.

"Ready to stretch my legs."

"We have to see Crystal now that you're with us, Manny. I want to make sure this marriage thing is going to work," Liz said, her brows pulled together in fake puzzlement.

"Don't you worry. This *marriage thing* is going to work," Manny said pulling Liz to him, and throwing a kiss to Jane in the rearview mirror.

Chapter 20

Cortez

It was seven in the morning. Mac and his crew had finished transferring the containers of shrimp from The Regina to his pickup truck. On the days Mac didn't skipper The Regina, Danny stepped in to help but, at the age of sixty-four, and with heavy drinking the night before, he wasn't much help. However, with the efforts of Mac's crew, they were making sure that money continued to come in.

Studs went on his way but Sissy and Shrimp accompanied Mac as he delivered the haul to various markets and then, as was their routine, stopped at Mac's mobile home to change his bandage. With the bandage task accomplished, Mac watched the two nurses jostle each other as they walked down the path to Sissy's truck.

Sipping the last of his coffee, he didn't move from the window until the truck was out of sight, returning his three wooded acres to the solitude he loved. His mind suddenly filled with his grandfather, a man he had loved, trusted, always felt safe with under his protective wing. The first Daniel Macintyre had purchased the piece of land, thinking someday he would tire of the sea and become a farmer, or, if he made it big, raise horses. Miraculously the property had stayed under the radar of the developers.

When Mac quit law school and took over as Captain of The Regina he moved out of the house and rented a room for a time near the docks. He threw his meager belongings into a couple of duffle bags along with a cigar box—the only thing he owned of his grandfather's.

He treasured the old cigar box and could still smell the smoke from when his grandfather told him of his adventures out at sea and the big one that got away. He still missed the old fisherman who died of a heart attack several years ago.

Unpacking his duffle bag, Mac had put away his few belongings in the sparsely furnished room—a bed, a three-drawer dresser, a table, a chair. He had sat on the bed, opened the cigar box, and found the forgotten property deed on the bottom, hidden by a newspaper clipping of the day a reporter snapped a picture of his grandfather proudly holding a big grouper: Winner of Saturday's Fishing Derby.

A few days later, he checked with pops about the piece of paper. Danny told his son, he had found the worthless document so it was his. Mac went straight to a real estate office, showed a young agent the deed and asked if it was real. At the time he didn't know that this was the first day the newly-licensed agent was on the job. The young woman, Florence Patterson, made a copy of the deed. It looked official to her and asked Mac to come back in a couple of days, give her time to check.

When he returned, Flo told him he was definitely a property owner—three acres of undeveloped land, some swamp, but mainly dense vegetation with a dirt road running along one side. She asked if he would like her to show him where the property was located.

He couldn't believe his good luck. The land was beautiful, lush, untouched. The next day he made a deal with the owner of one of the fish markets where he and his pops sold their fish. The man was selling a mobile home, a used trailer that was old but livable. He agreed to sell the trailer to Mac for a like amount of fish, but insisted it had to be red snapper. Mac shook hands, sealed the deal, but only after getting the fish monger to agree to haul the trailer the five miles to his property.

With Flo Patterson's help, he went to see the tax man for the county. It took the man several weeks to locate the records for the property and to calculate the amount owed since the last payment, which Mac said was the year his grandfather died. The man made a deal with Mac for monthly payments to bring the property taxes up to date.

Mac shook his head—so many memories of his grandfather. What would the old fisherman tell his grandson to do now? Mac turned from the window. He gingerly touched his arm. It had begun to feel sore the last few days. When Sissy removed the dressing, he noted since the stitches had been removed, there was redness around the scar tissue. It had been four weeks since his surgery and he thought he'd better not to take any chances of an infection setting in.

Mac was taking a tour boat out to see how it handled and to see if he took a liking to the tour business. With the day's schedule in place, he decided to check with Maria later.

His plans for the future were not jelling. He vacillated between things as they were, commercial fishing, versus sports fishing charters, versus tour boat charters. His physical therapist said because of the way he worked on his arm at the rehab center, he would be good as new in a few more weeks. Feeling time slipping by, pressure was on him to make a decision.

He had seen Maria once since their dinner date at the beach restaurant. It didn't go well. When she stepped into the restaurant he gave her a quick hug and guided her with his hand on the small of her back to the table where he had iced coffee waiting, his fingers warming as he touched her. Sitting across from each other he took her hand which felt so delicate in his rough calloused palm. She didn't withdraw, instead rested her other hand on top of his. Had she caressed his knuckles? He didn't know because her cell rang.

She listened, her brows drawing together at what was being said. "I'll be right there. Only a block away." She closed her cell. "Sorry, Mac, I have to run. Bad accident on 64. One dead. Multiple injuries. The ambulance is heading to the hospital."

Mac remembered giving her a quick kiss on her cheek and then she was gone.

So many memories—his grandfather, new ones of Maria—a feeling of melancholy swept over him.

Sighing, he changed into shorts, T-shirt, and rubber-soled boat shoes that had a grip if the deck of the boat became slippery. *Sure is different from long-line fishing,* he thought. "I can't imagine I'll take to it, but what the heck," he muttered. "See there, that's what a woman does. Screws with your head. Pops lost his love running away from the lonely life of a fisherman's wife. And, Mom, well, she certainly dotes on Pops, but I think she survives because when he's out of the house she can do her own thing. She has a life separate from his, he just doesn't realize it, or is happy to look the other way."

Chapter 21

The owner of the tour boat, a friend of Mac's, was more than happy to let the captain take out one of his Hurricane deck boats and especially when he only had a lone customer. It meant he had time for another cup of coffee, maybe even a plate of scrambled eggs and bacon while Mac was out. Mac, on the other hand, was eager to see how it felt—being on the water, talking about fishing without hauling them in. He had asked Shrimp and Sissy to come along to get their take on touring instead of fishing.

At 8:55 the lone passenger ambled up to the tour boat, waved and climbed aboard. He was ready to take the trip around the island.

"I'm Captain Mac," Mac said sticking out his hand. "Any place special you'd like to see this morning?" he asked pulling away from the dock.

"Name's Manny, Manny Salinas. My fiancé and her aunt were just getting up so I ducked out. However, I had to promise to tell them everything. They are an adventuresome pair. Might want to go out tomorrow."

"Fiancé, huh. Where you from?"

"East Coast. Port Orange. Liz and Jane, that's her aunt, are planning our wedding. Liz heard that beach weddings were big over here. We'll only have a few guests. Liz and I are pretty casual so it sounded great to me. Not one for all that hoopla that a guy can get entangled with."

"Know what you mean."

The men stood side by side slowly cruising up the Intracoastal Waterway to the north end of Anna Maria Island.

"That's the old pier over there. If you're walking around and see a trolley sign and a bench, wait a few minutes and one will come along, pick you up, drop you off at shops, nice little cafes and that pier." The warm breeze from the boat rippled Mac's curly forelock to the side under his ball cap.

Manny also wore a ball cap. He had retired the month before but his body was still wired as a cop. He had pulled on his black jeans and T-shirt this morning before Liz had a chance to talk him into shorts. Because Jane was with them, they opted for a two-bedroom suite. They didn't fool Aunt Jane. She knew when Liz crept out from the bed beside hers where the woman was going, and it wasn't to play checkers.

"You married?" Manny asked taking a sip of coffee.

Sissy and Shrimp were in the back of the boat, noses stuck up into the warmth of the morning sun. They weren't sure what to expect when Mac asked them to come along. Studs was going to join them but decided to stay on shore, get some sleep, and then hopefully end up in the arms of the luscious barmaid he met before going out shrimping the night before.

"No. Too busy. Those two back there are my crew. They help me with The Regina. We're commercial fishermen."

"I hear that's one of the most dangerous professions ... maybe even before cops."

"Yeah, it can be. Tore up my arm a few weeks back."

"Will you still be able to fish?" Manny asked.

"Sure. Could slow me down but ... actually thinking ahead ... well, that's the reason I'm out on this tour boat thing. But I'm thinking there's not enough action. We fishermen aren't exactly big talkers ... you know, alone out at sea. Maybe I should trade in my fishing boat, The Regina, as a down payment for a sports fishing boat, a charter. Or maybe do the charter thing and keep The Regina. I could be a regular corporation. What do they call it, two money streams?"

Mac took a look at his passenger as he took off his cap, scratched his scalp then pulled it back covering his brush cut, the bill shading his eyes behind dark glasses from the glare of the sun off the water. "You a policeman?"

"Was. Started in Albuquerque. Spent the last ten years in Daytona Beach. Just retired. Liz, hope you get to meet her, is a private investigator. Started her own business. That's how we met. Well, one thing led to another … we fell in love." Manny shook his head, a smile creeping across his face thinking about his fiery redhead. "And, we decided to work together, go into business together. I specialize more in cyber stuff. Stitch—"

"Stitch?"

Manny chuckled. "Yeah, Elizabeth Stitchway. She says she's one of those modern women. Going to keep her maiden name as far as clients go. Any who, she investigates anything that comes her way … actually, we both do."

"Manny … okay if I call you Manny?"

"Only if I can drop the captain and call you Mac?" Manny said smiling. "Anymore coffee on this ship?"

"Ah, boat talk."

"I live on a houseboat … ex navy."

"Help yourself. Thermos in that bag next to your seat. Here's my cup. Fill her up. Black."

Manny was enjoying himself. Beautiful morning, a tryst with Liz last night, and now a new friend. *Doesn't get any better than this,* he thought returning with two full mugs of coffee. Black.

Cruising around the northern tip of the island, Mac continued his banter about the types of fish he and his crew catch as commercial fishermen, the number of days they spend at sea before bringing them in, and then unloading the catch at the fish houses.

"Mac, can you point out the Sandbar restaurant when we pass? That's were Liz and Jane are meeting the event planner about our wedding."

"Great place. It's up ahead. Lots of weddings there. If I were ever to get married … and I'm not …. I'd like it there. There's an old church—Roser Community Church—also, beautiful. My pops …"

Manny looked at Mac. He hadn't finished his sentence. *I bet something happened at that church,* Manny surmised. *And from the faraway look on the captain's face, I don't think it was pleasant.*

"You were saying about your dad?"

"What? Lost my train of thought … a weird incident that happened to my doctor. Dr. Maria Grayson. Kinda weird, I don't know what else to call it. I had a nasty gash—she patched me up. It's still healing."

Manny stole a glance at the man at the wheel. He'd switched from talking about his dad to talking about his doctor. Speaking of his doctor he seemed to relax after saying the pops word. *Something going on with the doctor-patient thing.*

"Sure. Fire away. I see lots of weird stuff."

"Well, she told me about a big lawyer," Mac chuckled throwing a smile at Manny. "Anyway, she said that this man in a suit walks up to her at the hospital. Said he had been looking for her and introduces himself. Said he was a lawyer from New Orleans working a case. Said that he was investigating the death of a patient. This lawyer guy was desperately trying to find someone, an eyewitness to some skullduggery that happened at the hospital where Maria was a resident."

"Your doctor, Dr. Grayson, did she see something?"

"Well, that's the weird part. She remembers the day, remembers pausing at the door to the room, but nothing else. I'm not sure if she just doesn't want to remember. Maybe feeling guilty for not helping. But I'm thinking if a lawyer tracks her down, maybe something did happen, something bad and he wants to pin it on her. This lawyer had come up with her name. She was a resident surgeon scheduled that day on the floor of the guy that turned up dead. Manny, she didn't bat an eyelash when she told Bennett, that's the lawyer, that she saw nothing unusual when she was on duty. Nothing that could be termed skullduggery that is. She's telling me this story and I sense something is wrong ... Maria had switched back from a friend to a professional doctor, if you know what I mean."

Manny knew what he meant. This man had feelings for his doctor.

"Hey, Skipper, manatee, starboard." Sissy called out.

"I see it. Manny, there, over there," Mac said pointing off the starboard side.

"Big guy," Manny said snapping a picture with his cell.

"Did you ever find out what was bothering you about what she said?"

"Not really. She saw a man in a white coat over pin-striped pants, and remembers the room number, 313."

"She remembered the room number?"

"Said she'll never forget ... unlucky thirteen. Do you think she's liable for anything? It's been two years."

"Has this Bennett fella been back?"

"Not that I know of, haven't asked her but I have a feeling he will be. It's been a few weeks. Could she be in danger?"

"Probably not, but it depends on who the dead man was. If it was murder… did the lawyer say what he thought happened?"

"Again, not that I know of. Maria said that a nurse told her later that the man in 313 pulled his IV out."

"Strange. Could be murder. Could be, if the lawyer found your doctor, the killer could want to silence her. If Dr. Grayson knows the man's name, the one who died or at least the day and approximate time, I'll snoop around and see if I can come up any reason someone would want to kill him, the dead guy."

"Oh, Maria knows … maybe not the name … but I'm sure the date."

"Tell you what, if the good doctor wants to give you the date, time, hospital, why don't you and she meet us for dinner tonight at the Sandbar. Here's my business card with my cell. Liz and Jane will be talking non-stop about the wedding plans so I'm sure we can get your business done. Besides, I'd like to meet this Maria of yours. 7:30 okay?"

Chapter 22

Wally ambled into the Cortez Kitchen Restaurant and Bar behind two other guys, one in cutoffs and the other in jeans and yellow T-shirt. Cutoffs turned to his right returning the wave of a threesome sitting in the middle of the array of picnic tables. Yellow-shirt looked around then took a seat at the bar. Wally climbed up on the empty barstool in the corner next to the yellow shirt. Wally had watched him for the last two days and knew the guy had an eye for women.

Yellow-shirt leaned in, ordered a beer, and then swung around to listen to the band. Wally pointed to the bottle the bartender set down for yellow-shirt, nodding he'd like one of the same.

It was 8:30. The sun low in the sky. The beachy outdoor atmosphere merging with the inside was casual dining at its best. The band, pony-tailed guys in jeans and T-shirts strumming guitars, banging drums, one of them fingering a harmonica, let the music rip from the stage out to enthusiastic fans. Fans sat at tables or the bar, or stood to the side. Some relaxed on boats tied to pilings holding the deck holding the spillover crowd … keeping the beat alive.

Wally grinned at the scene: rustic décor set in the middle of the historic fishing village of Cortez. It looked like a shack on the outside but the chef was serious about serving the freshest fish to his hungry patrons after a day sunning on the beach or a day of fishing out in the Gulf. Wally breathed deep of the salt air on the brisk breeze rolling in through the three open sides of the bar surrounded by fishing boats and a commercial boatyard.

The waitresses dressed in tight jeans and T-shirts darted table to table over the rough-hewn floorboards replacing empty bottles of beer and cocktail glasses with another round of drinks. Yup, Wally was enjoying his current assignment.

The band finished the set to stamping feet, hands slapping thighs, and was immediately replaced with lively chatter but muted in the corner for which Wally was grateful. He had a proposition for Yellow-shirt, one that couldn't be shouted.

"Hey, Studs, sitting at the bar? I can't serve you there."

"Later, sugar lips. You find me a seat at a table and I'm all yours."

"Later." Sugar lips smiled promising her favorite customer he would receive her full attention as she brushed his thigh with her arm and scurried off balancing a tray of empties.

Chuckling, Studs swung back to his beer.

Wally chuckled with him, "Gotta luv the honies."

"That you do, bro. That you do."

"Nice spot … any suggestions for a late bite to eat?"

"Grouper Rubin. Don't pass it up. You visiting?" Studs asked.

"Business. But I like to mix a little pleasure with business," Wally said raising the bottle of beer to his lips.

"I hear you. Business always intruding on the pleasure it seems. I'm on my way for a night of shrimping." Studs swallowed the last of his bottle, tapped the empty on the bar, asking for another.

"Oh, that sounds like hard work … that kind of business. Ever think of doing something else? Something that would allow you and Miss Sugar Lips to hide away on an island between jobs?"

"Fat chance. Is that what you do? Island hopping with a dame?"

"Sometimes. It's getting harder … too much to do. That's why I'm here … looking for help."

"Like what do you do?"

"A little of this … little of that. Mostly boring detective work … making sure others are doing what they're supposed to be doing."

"Any special training?"

"Naw … on the job. Just have to pay attention to detail, and if the boss says he needs you, you have to tell Sugar Lips that you'll be gone for a few days. Hell, you can go back to a blonde sugar lips, or find a redhead. I can see you pay attention to detail." Wally and Studs chuckled as they both watched Miss Sugar Lips strut by.

"If you're interested, we can meet, share a couple of joints if you're into it. I'm working on a big score now and could use someone who pays attention to detail. When the job is done you can take Sugar to one of the islands ... hang out until the next score."

"Hey, Junior?"

"Yeah. Did you come up with a plan? I'm hearing some unsettling rants from the guys in New Orleans. May have to make a move. Don't want to take a chance on a certain woman suddenly changing her mind about what she thinks she didn't see."

"Not *a* plan, Junior. Two plans—A, and if that doesn't work then I'll put my sure-fire plan B into action."

"Watch out, Wally. You might get A and B mixed up. You don't do well with complications. Has that lawyer been to see the doctor again?"

"Once. Met in the hospital's chapel. But there was an emergency of some kind and she couldn't have said more than hello and raced out. Good thing because I didn't have a chance to bug the place."

"Keep on it."

Chapter 23

Anna Maria Island

A storm was brewing far out in the gulf. The wait staff at the Sandbar, as well as the evening diners, kept a furtive eye at the streaks of lightning off in the distance. Sultry air swirled softly around the tables but the gusts lacked strength. Strangely the storm seemed to be kept at bay. For the moment.

Crystal relaxed at her usual table enjoying a shrimp cocktail unconcerned by the approaching storm.

Manny, with Jane and Liz on his arms, entered the restaurant, their new long sundresses fluttering in the breeze, and freshly pedicured toes peeking out from under the hems—cherry red for Liz; purple with silver sequins for Jane.

Before selecting a table, Manny looked around for Mac. When Mac brought Manny ashore earlier, he found Maria was scheduled at the hospital so he asked his mother to join them. Regina eagerly accepted. It wasn't often that her son asked her out to dinner.

Spotting Crystal, Jane urged Manny and Liz to select a table off the patio so they could put their bare feet in the soft sand while she said hello to her friend.

"Crystal, nice to see you," Jane squealed plunking down on the empty chair alongside the psychic. "Liz and I are here with her fiancé,

Manny. I'll bring them over later so you can meet them. Looks like nasty weather heading our way, Hope we have time for dinner."

"Not to worry, Jane. There's plenty of time. Ooops, oh my," Crystal exclaimed.

As Mac and Regina passed the table to join Manny and Liz several tables away on the sand, Crystal's wine glass skipped an inch, swayed, and toppled over. Jane jumped up dabbing a napkin on the spilled white wine but Crystal didn't move. Her eyes were glued to the older woman who had just swished by in the direction of Liz and Manny. Manny obviously knew the gentleman as he stood and shook the man's hand. Crystal watched the interchange that ensued, apparently introductions.

"Crystal, who are you looking at?" Jane asked.

Crystal squinted, nodded, nodded again. Jane followed the track of Crystal's eyes.

"Oh, that must be the man and his mother that Manny told us about. He's a fisherman, or was … or still is," Jane said looking over her shoulder. "Anyway, he took Manny out on a tour around the island this morning. Crystal, what's the matter with you. You look like you saw a ghost."

"That woman. Jane, you and Liz must get something personal or at the very least, something she touches—glass, fork. Whatever you can. Bring it over tonight. Must be tonight. It's the storm. The woman. Promise me you'll come. I don't care what time."

"Yes, but it might—"

Jane didn't finish her sentence. Crystal laid a twenty-dollar bill on the table, sat the saltshaker on top of the bill and fled away down the beach.

Liz looked up as Jane approached the table. Her aunt had a gleam in her eye. With a slight nod at the fleeing Crystal, Jane grasped her niece's arm. "Excuse us for just a minute, folks. We'll be right back."

Jane hustled from the table steering Liz in front of her, rounded the corner into the darkness of the bushes.

"Aunt Jane, for heaven's sake, what's wrong with you?"

"Who's the woman at our table?"

"Regina Macintyre. She's Captain Mac's mother. Mac is—"

"I know, I know, the man who took Manny out for a tour this morning. When she passed Crystal and me, Crystal was spooked and, Liz, her wine glass walked on the table and then toppled over. It was scary. Then Crystal implored me to bring you and Manny, but more important to bring something to her tonight that *that woman* had touched. She doesn't care what time but practically ordered us to see her tonight. I tell you, Lizzie, I wouldn't take a chance on her casting a spell over us. When we go back to the table, let me sit next to the woman and don't say anything if I do something crazy. Come on, dear."

Jane didn't wait for Liz to respond, again taking Liz's arm, steering her out of the bushes to the table. Jane plunked down in the empty seat between Manny and Regina. Then Mac played musical chairs moving over next to Manny with introductions all around.

Manny leaned in to Liz. "Everything okay?"

Liz rolled her eyes. Said nothing.

Then it was Manny's turn to shuffle the deck. He stood and invited Mac to come to the bar with him. He had a special drink he thought the ladies might like but had to see if the bartender had the liquors to concoct the drink.

At the bar, Mac slipped Manny a piece of paper. "Maria gave me the information you asked for—hospital, date, time, and verified the room number—313. She also said the dead guy's name was Arturo Perez."

Manny pocketed the paper and the two men returned to the table.

Liz looked up as Manny sat down. "Where's the incredible, super delicious drink you wanted for us ladies?" she asked.

"Oh, the waitress is bringing a carafe of white wine. I was sure you and Jane were going to order a fish entre. You are aren't you?" Manny asked.

"Probably, but, Regina, how about you?" Liz asked.

"Yeah, Mom. Fish or steak? I can order a different wine—"

"I'm going to have their pork medallions but white wine is fine, I assure you," Regina whispered, quietly spitting the words into Mac's ear and then turned smiling at her other dinner companions.

Conversation centered around the tour Mac had given Manny—the beauty of the island, the manatee Sissy had spotted, and a dolphin that followed alongside the boat for a few yards. And, yes, the captain pointed out the Sandbar restaurant and the beach where Manny planned to make Liz his wife.

Jane glanced around the table. Everyone had finished their dinner and were discussing dessert when the waitress hustled over to remove the empty plates. Jane hadn't made her move. Liz could feel her aunt tensing up, her lips pierced in a thin line and her chest was rising and falling at an alarming rate. The waitress leaned in to remove Regina's plate and while her arm was in mid air Jane reached for her water glass, missed and bumped the young girl's arm. The empty dinner plate with a smidge of pork, the knife, fork, and plate fell into Jane's lap. Jane deftly covered the knife with a fold of her dress helping the waitress to retrieve the rest back onto her tray.

Chapter 24

Angry black clouds let loose torrents of rain as fierce winds slammed the raindrops like pellets against the three people hustling from the car to Crystal's front door.

Jane rapped the big brass knocker three times.

Creaking, the door swung open. Then the door silently shut behind the visitors after they stepped inside. Crystal had lit numerous candles around the room the flickering flames casting shadows throughout the still air.

"Give it to me," Crystal commanded in a hushed voice extending her hand to Jane.

"Yes, yes, here," Jane said fishing the dirty knife from her shoulder bag.

"Sit, everyone," Crystal whispered as she slid onto the cushion of the black chair.

Crystal placed the knife between her palms the blade extending beyond her fingers glinting in the candlelight. She closed her eyes and touched the handle, her index finger sliding to the blade, and then sharply pulling her fingers away. The knife dropped to the table. "This knife is surrounded with evil," she pronounced.

Suddenly the double window behind Liz and Jane blew open. The wind howled through the opening extinguishing all the candles but the one in the middle of the table. Liz and Jane saw Crystal's head snap up, her eyes open wide. They turned to see what she was staring at, sucking in a breath, "Oh, oh," they said simultaneously clutching each other. "Do you see that? Manny, do you see that?" Jane whispered.

Manny didn't answer or didn't hear, he was on his feet sprinting to the window. Pulled the left side shut, pushed down the bolt, then the right side, the billowing white curtain falling still.

"It's the ghost bride," Crystal murmured. "The bride's crying. Rushing here. The knife, the knife is gone."

"Nonsense. Where's the light switch?" Manny asked feeling around in the dark.

Crystal didn't speak.

Manny felt along the wall near the door, found the switch and turned on the lights. He and Liz glanced at the empty table. They both dropped to their knees, crawled under the table searching side to side, around the chairs and the legs of the two women rooted in their seats.

They found nothing.

"Must have blown off under one of those cabinets and we're not going to move them tonight." Manny, hands on his hips, exchanged eye contact with Liz.

Leaving the house, Manny helped Jane into the backseat of the car, then turned to Liz. "What did you see?"

"I don't know," Liz mumbled. "Crystal seemed to think the white curtains … a bride?"

Back at the motel Liz kissed Manny good night whispering, "Given the scare Jane had, I'd better go right to bed with her."

"Okay, but I'll leave the adjoining door open."

"Good idea," Liz whispered.

The wind continued to howl as Liz snuggled into her bed. Jane pulled the cover to her chin in the bed next to Liz, both staring at the ceiling trying to settle their nerves.

The window flew up. The blinds banged against the frame. The gauze curtains billowed out.

Jane and Liz screamed.

Manny raced into the room and pulled the window shut. The white sheer curtain stopped billowing, falling limp over the panes of glass.

Liz jumped into Jane s bed.

GumDrop, back arched, hackles raised, continued hissing at the filmy curtain.

"Manny, stay in here, please. For Aunt Jane. I'm fine mind you," Liz said.

Manny climbed into the bed Liz had occupied pulling the sheet up over his chest. Jane and Liz had the coverlet up to their chins peering at the limp curtain. GumDrop stopped hissing. Settling down in her carrier, she fell asleep.

"Manny, can we leave for Port Orange now?"

"Go to sleep, Stitch. We'll leave in the morning as planned."

Chapter 25

Tapping her foot on the floor pushing the swing to a gentle sway, Maria stared absentmindedly out at the Gulf. Her cell, lying on the cushion beside her, rang.

"Dr. Grayson? Ross Bennett here. Can we meet at your home—ten o'clock? You know, away from prying eyes?"

"You haven't called since we met at the chapel ... not a meeting really since I was called to the OR." Maria sighed. "I'd prefer that too, at my home ... if we have to meet." Maria gave him her address and told him she'd call if she saw a problem develop.

"I'm bringing someone with me. I told him about you, and, well, he said he wanted to be with me when we chatted next."

"Who?"

"Someone I've worked with before. He handles criminal investigations in Louisiana, actually, many of the southern states. We'll see you tomorrow."

The line disconnected and Maria laid the cell back on the cushion. *Serious. This is serious.* "Maybe I shouldn't meet them here. Dumb move, Grayson," she mumbled. "Meeting two men in your home, by yourself. I checked Bennett out. He's a lawyer in New Orleans but now another man purported to be a police officer."

Padding to the kitchen she retrieved a frozen lasagna dinner and popped it into the microwave. Waiting for the timer to ding, she retrieved her cell and called Mac.

"Hey, sweetheart, Bogie here."

"How's the arm?"

"Hanging in there."

"Mac—not funny. Any problems? I haven't heard from you … I thought you'd call."

"I know … I'll tell you later … I've been busy."

"Busy?"

"Yeah … trying to figure out what I want to be when I grow up, what I want to do with my life," he replied forcing a chuckle.

"I see. I'd be interested in hearing … about what you want to do with your life. But right now I'm calling to ask a favor."

"Name it."

"Could you help me out tomorrow about ten in the morning? Oh, no, that's not good. Will you be fishing?"

"The crew can take The Regina out. As I've said before, 'no fish, no money. Now, tell me what happened. You sound … well, I don't know. But you don't sound right."

"Ross Bennett called. He wants to meet with me. Mac, it must be serious because he said he could be here by ten and that he was bringing an officer with him."

"What kind of an officer?"

"Oh, I didn't ask. I presumed a police officer. Anyway, I got to thinking that it wasn't too bright to meet them here alone. Can you meet them with me?"

"Sure. You fix the coffee, and I'll bring bagels with cream cheese. All pricey lawyers like cream cheese, and police officers practically live on bagels. That's what I hear anyway."

"Mac, I don't think this is a social visit."

Chapter 26

At 9:30 a.m. Mac pulled into the tree-lined driveway of the beach house that Maria was tending. He was not prepared for the woman who answered the door. He'd seen her in various colored scrubs and a sundress. The woman in front of him had on low-cut jeans and a white T-shirt that followed her curves from her neck to her ankles. While taking in the outline of her body it was the intensity of her eyes that really grabbed him. The violet had turned almost black and there was a worried furrow between her brows. This woman was troubled. No, she was scared and she was trying to hide it.

He stepped through the door pushing it shut with his foot as he pulled her against him, his bad arm dangling at his side, fingers clasping a white paper bag. There was no hesitation in her response. In his arms was exactly where she wanted to be and to Mac, it was exactly where he wanted her to be. *Oh, God, I'm in trouble,* he thought. He could feel the pounding of her heart. Was she frightened or was her heart responding to him? He didn't know and didn't care. He just knew it felt good. Felt right.

Pulling back, he held her chin up and looked into those wide eyes. "Hey, everything's going to be okay."

"Thanks for coming, Mac," she said pulling away, pulling a strand of her auburn hair behind her ears. "I'm sorry. I didn't mean to accost you. It's just … why is Bennett bringing an officer?"

The doorbell rang.

Maria looked up sharply but didn't move.

"We'll know soon, sweetheart." Mac turned, opened the door to find two startled men dressed in nondescript gray suits, white shirts, both with black and white striped ties. They had expected a woman to answer not a muscled bodyguard

Maria appeared beside Mac and nodded for the men to enter. Mac moved to her side one arm resting easily around her shoulders, the other at his side holding the sack.

"I asked my friend to meet with us. After all," Maria tried to laugh but nothing came out, "I'm alone and—"

"Maria, not a problem. This is Agent Alex Donovan, FBI. Dr. Maria Grayson and—"

"Mac Macintyre." Mac stepped forward and shook the agent's hand.

Maria stood rooted to the floor. *An FBI agent.*

"Mac, this is Ross Bennett, the lawyer I told you about," Maria said in low voice.

"Mr. Bennett." Mac nodded extending his hand. "Okay, gentlemen, let's get this over with. I know that Dr. Grayson has duties at the hospital."

"There's a table out in the screened porch." Maria said glancing at the briefcases in the men's hands. "It's this way."

They followed Maria walking in back of the swing, walking in back of the curved couch, and through a door into an oasis of greenery—a lovely screened dining area with the soft sound of waves lapping the nearby shore.

Bennett and Donovan walked to the far side—Mac and Maria stood facing them. The line was drawn.

Maria found her voice. "My manners. Coffee anyone? Mac?" she asked stepping to the end of the table where she had set plates, knives, and a carafe of coffee. Mac set the white sack next to the plates and Maria placed the contents in a basket, then pushed the plunger on the carafe passing the mugs of coffee along to her guests.

"Your arm, Mr. Macintyre. That's quite a lump under the white sleeve." Agent Donovan was the first to speak a bleak attempt to break the tension.

"Fishing accident. Dr. Grayson fixed me up. A few more weeks and I'll get this wretched thing off." Mac smiled accepting the mug of coffee, set it on the table and briefly squeezed Maria's hand a gesture letting her know that he was with her.

Mac's actions were not lost on Bennett and Donovan. It was obvious there was a relationship consisting of more than some stitches and a band aid. They pulled yellow-lined pads of paper from their briefcases and Bennett set a recorder in the center of the glass table. A blue jay cawed from a branch in a nearby tree. A gecko ran up the screen, stopped, his neck pumping, looking at the people on the other side.

Maria shot a glance at Mac. This was all so perfunctory, could have been anybody, any guests she was having over for a coffee klatch, but they weren't just anyone, and they weren't guests. They were all business.

"We're going to record our conversation. Is that all right with you?" Bennett asked.

Maria nodded, yes. Picked up her coffee and took a sip. Mac noticed a slight tremor in her fingers which relaxed as she held the hot mug. He hadn't seen this before. The professional, the doctor who had faced much worse on a metal table, white mask over her nose and mouth.

"Maria, may I call you Maria?" Donovan asked.

She nodded yes.

"Ross called me. Told me he had done further investigating," Donovan said. "I'd like to hear what you saw … in your own words, Maria."

Maria stood, walked to the end of the table staring through the screen at the water beyond. Without turning to the men, she related what she had seen. Repeating what she had told Mac while having drinks at the restaurant. The same story she had told Ross. She had seen a man in a white coat and striped pants bending over a patient.

"Do you think you could identify the man if you saw a picture of him?" Donovan asked.

Maria swung around. "First, Mr. Donovan—"

"Alex," the agent said with a warm smile.

"First, Alex, why are you here? Why the FBI?"

The agent exchanged glances with Ross then reached over turning the recorder off.

"The man you saw murdered—"

"I never said I saw him being murdered," Maria said, her voice tense as she sat down by Mac.

"That man was Arturo Perez, head of a smuggling cartel in Ciudad Juarez which he ran from Louisiana," Donovan said, his voice a monotone. He could have been describing a loaf of bread. "His operation smuggled drugs as well as guns into Texas, where they had runners who distributed what came across the border to other runners into many of our southern states and north. We, the FBI, have been investigating Perez for some time. His son, Juan Perez took over the family business. But he is not the leader his father was."

"Who would want to kill Perez" Mac topped off his coffee. The others declined.

"Ross and I have had many discussions on this topic, Mr. Macintyre. Juan Perez was born in the States so perhaps he wanted to take over the business. We're investigating that angle. These are bad, ruthless people who will stop at nothing. Arturo Perez wanted to merge all southern drug smuggling gangs under his rule. With his death, we think we have a chance to round up, prosecute the top members from California to Florida—cut off the head of the snake, if we can find out who killed Perez."

Donovan leaned back in his chair, looked at Bennett, then back to Maria—his words hanging in the still, humid air.

Ross sipped his coffee then leaned forward. "Maria, with your description of the man you saw in room 313 removing the IV from Arturo Perez's arm, you will be a pivotal witness. By all indications he knew removing the IV will sound an alarm. The nurse found it turned off and swears she didn't turn the machine off. Your testimony would be so important, that ... well, Alex you tell her."

"I want to escort you to a safe house immediately, put you under our witness protection program, give you a new identity and—"

"This is preposterous. Your assumptions are wrong. I saw nothing. Definitely not a murder. Other than what I've told you ... what the man was wearing ... I would never be able to identify him ... pieces of clothing. You came here for nothing. And, I'm not going anywhere. This is my life. I've worked hard for the position I hold in the hospital," Maria snapped.

Wow, Mac thought. *If Donovan thought Maria was going to go along with him he didn't know that this delicate looking woman was made of steel. Donovan had grossly misjudged his star witness.*

Maria stood. "This meeting is over. I told Mr. Bennett and now I'm telling you, Agent Donovan, I saw nothing!"

Wally lost her and Junior was steamed that he hadn't eliminated the problem.

What was he to do? He couldn't be in two places at once—the hospital and her home in hopes of somehow picking up her trail. She didn't show up at the hospital for the beginning of her shift this morning. Maybe she was sick. He doubled back to her house, parking in the driveway of a snowbird couple who had flown north to beat Florida's summer heat.

There were two cars parked in her driveway.

"Now what?" Wally muttered. "Maybe it's my lucky day or maybe she's having a stupid brunch for her friends."

Slouching down in the car, his eyes drooped with fatigue as he watched the stairs leading up to the front door of the house.

The door opened. Two men stepped out. Wally's eyes were trained on the men as they trotted down the steps, got into one of the cars and drove away. One of the men was that lawyer Bennett. He was sure of it. But who was the other man?

The front door opened again. A man stood beside Maria, hugged her briefly which resulted in a very warm kiss, and then he left in the remaining car. Wally grinned. He knew who this man was. He was her patient. He'd seen her in his hospital room and again at the restaurant when he recorded her telling him what she had seen, which was nothing. Wally had inquired, found out the man was in the hospital because of a freak accident—a fisherman with a gimpy arm.

So, the patient is becoming a close friend, very close. Well, he'd be easy to get rid of. No way he could come to her rescue. Not with that arm.

Chapter 27

Cortez

It was Friday, the middle of a very hot summer. The day dawned with a brilliant sun over the West Coast of Florida. Tourists and residents alike were getting ready to party, ready to leave the constant chatter from news reporters regarding another terrorist attack, stock markets diving, and world economies tanking.

The pristine white beaches swelled from a few sunbathers to a throng of colorful umbrellas, scantily clad young women and children shrieking with glee as another wave lapped over their toes.

Mac grinned as his plan jelled under the morning sun.

He hoped that Maria had enough seniority so that she'd be free unless the ER was overwhelmed. He had a couple of ulterior motives for calling her. Well, maybe even three. First he wanted to see her. The day he came to her home to be with her when the lawyer and the FBI agent came calling haunted him. He could still feel her body pressed against him, the scent of her hair, and his increasing need to protect her. And, he wanted to see how she was handling her decision about not letting the agent put her in protective custody. And, he wanted to see what kind of a seaman she was.

And then there was his struggle with the growing knowledge that his fishing days seemed to be crashing to an end. He thought more and more about how he could still keep his love, hell, his passion for the sea, how he was going to adapt to what he faced with his arm's diminished capacity. *After all, wasn't that what I was thinking when I took Manny out for a tour, or maybe joining the growing ranks of the sports fishing guys? I know I could do it with at least one strong crewman. I think I can handle it ... give it a good try.*

But this morning Mac sat behind the wheel of the old Hurricane Deck Boat, the same boat he took Manny out on. She wasn't too bad. Nice white paint job, new dark blue Bimini top over the side benches and another that he could swing up to cover the captain when needed for protection from the sun, or a passenger sitting next to him.

With his fingers tracing the wheel's polished wood. His back to the dock gazing at the rippling water, a smile crossed Mac's face as he thought of Maria. *It was time to call her, ask her if she would take a tour with him,* he thought pulling his cell from his pants pocket.

"Hi, sweetheart," Mac said looking up at the picnic tables on the dock.

"Good morning. Beautiful day." Maria said padding to her favorite spot on the swing. If she admitted it, she was thrilled to hear Mac's husky voice.

"Are you up for a picnic? I'm taking my crew out on a tour boat. It's a perfect day and Sissy has packed a terrific lunch under Shrimp's guidance. Studs might join us unless a waitress smiles at him. Mind you not a particular waitress—any waitress. When we dock we'll leave them to their own weekend celebrations and you and I will go somewhere for a nice private dinner. What do you say?"

"Sounds like fun. What time and where do I meet you?"

"Come down to The Star Fish Market dock. Can't miss it there are signs as you come over the bridge. Some seats on the boat have a cover overhead so you can take your pick—sun or shade. As for when, as soon as possible. I'll be waiting for you."

Chapter 28

The woman in white—shorts, T-shirt, sandals, topped with a straw hat—strolled down the dock. Heads turned, men and women alike. Mac waved, then watched as a smile spread across her face, the pace of her footsteps increasing. Maria's thick auburn hair was pulled back, anchored with a white ribbon at the nape of her neck.

He could have kissed his two crewmen who, after hearing that Maria was going to join the tour, suddenly had things to do. Sissy and Shrimp chuckled as they clamored out of the Hurricane wishing their skipper a fun day.

Mac extended his hand to steady Maria as she stepped onto the boat.

"Where's your crew? You said—"

"I know ... they had things to do. I wasn't about to stop them. You look wonderful," he said, planting a quick kiss on her lips. "Now, for a tour. Look to the front—"

"That would be the bow. I do know a little ... and," turning her head over her other shoulder, "that would be the stern. And," nudging a cooler under the bench with her sandal, "would be lunch. Poor guys. They forgot their picnic in their haste to leave."

Mac shrugged, eyebrows raised, as he started the engine. "Here, sit in front of me. The captain's seat is high so he can point out places of interest to his tourist ... that would be you. I pulled up the second cover so the sun won't be in our eyes, plus I don't want you to get burned the first time I take you out for a cruise."

Maria settled on the seat in front of Mac as he carefully pulled away from the dock, waved to another skipper bringing a group of tourists in for an early lunch at the Star Fish Market's outside food bar.

Clear of the dock and into the bay Mac pushed on the accelerator and the Hurricane picked up speed leaving a wake of sparkling water in the sunshine. Maria grabbed for her hat in the nick of time as the wind from the boat cutting through the air lifted the brim. Laughing, she rolled it up and tucked it in her tote.

"We'll run out a ways. There's a sandbar I want to show you. The tide is out so we can ease up, drop anchor, and look for seashells."

Neither spoke enjoying the cool air on their faces. Mac leaned forward, pointing over her shoulder to the right. A manatee had surfaced, looked at the boat heading its way and disappeared under a wave.

Maria looked up, raised her arm, her finger pointing to a pelican as it dived into the water for lunch. The large bird surfaced and flew off with a fish hanging out either side of its long beak.

Spotting a shady area along a spit of land Mac eased up on the gas, then cut the engine, the forward motion nudging the Hurricane up on the narrow beach.

Maria stood, turned to look at Mac. "This doesn't look like a sandbar, Captain."

"You're right, First Mate. But, it is a nice spot for lunch and I'm starved. Then we go to the sandbar. Okay with you, sweetheart?"

"Absolutely."

"I'll get out first," Mac said. "Hand me the cooler and then put your hands on my shoulders for support. The boat's bouncing a little."

"You have this picnic thing all figured out, Bogie," she said as they ambled up the short beach to a grassy spot next to a bank of palmetto bushes.

"Okay, let's take a look at what the boys selected for lunch. Ah huh … three beers. No wine. Sorry."

"Stop complaining. Hand me a couple of bottles and I'll screw off the caps. Just to let you know I have a bottle of water in my tote."

"And, there's more water in a cooler under a bench up front. Now, let's see. Ah, yes, three sandwiches on rye. Don't know what kind until we unwrap them … and some pickles. Should tide us over for a while," Mac said handing Maria a sandwich in exchange for a beer. Tapping his bottle to hers he said, "Here's to a happy tour."

"It already is my friend. I'm glad you called." Maria leaned forward. Kissed his cheek.

Mac put his sandwich down, traced the side of her face … then slowly over her lips. His hand gently circled behind her neck pulling her mouth to his. He tasted mustard … more mustard. His lips lingered, her mouth warm, inviting.

Reluctantly, Mac pulled away, only a little, so he could see her eyes. They were closed. He kissed each lid.

Her eyes still closed, she whispered, "Thanks for inviting me … to your picnic." Her eyes flew open, crinkled at the corners. "When do I get to look for seashells?"

"Soon. Do you see that change in the color of the water," he asked pointing off to his right.

"Oh, yes … but you said sand. Looks like light-blue water then it changes to a darker blue."

"The sand's there. The tide's coming in barely covering it … the sandbar will disappear. Seamen who don't know the waters around here can beach their boats depending on the depth of the hull."

"Mac, what about your arm. You can't let it get wet."

"Not to worry, sweetheart. Under the Captain's seat is a beautiful blue sleeve that this crazy doctor prescribed for me. Let's pack up and we'll be on our way—less than ten minutes."

The Hurricane's bow was designed with a rail that slid back. Mac scooted off the end, blue sleeve in place. He gave Maria a hand as she sat on the end slipping off beside him. The water warmed by the hot sand covered Maria's toes, and after a few steps, near the edge, circled her ankles before the deeper drop off.

"Mac, look … look at this. A conch and he's …

"He's home. Here … a sea urchin." Mac gentle placed the small creature on her palm. "Watch. His spiny needles move. He's alive. And, over there … a sand-dollar. See the tiny fingers on the outer edge? Makes it look fuzzy. Watch … the fingers will move showing you it's alive."

"I've read you should never pick up a shell until you can tell if it's alive or dead." Maria knelt in the water, watching to see if the sand-dollar's fingers were moving.

"That's right. Look at this one, a Cockle shell."

"Oh, I've seen those in craft shops," Maria said tracing the ribs of the shell gently with her finger.

"My grandfather said they are sometimes called Heart Clams because if you look at the shell from the side, it has a heart shape."

Maria tucked a Heart Clam in her pocket as they turned, slowly walking through the rising water to the boat. The water had inched higher allowing the boat to bob against the anchor. Maria hiked up sitting on the edge of the deck.

"Your grandfather sounds like he was a very sweet person," Maria said.

Mac glanced up, caught the warmth in her violet eyes. Desire welled inside of him. He wanted her ... wanted her for a lifetime ... to hell with what he could offer her ... he'd make her happy, somehow ...

Maria put her arms around his neck, her legs twining around his waist.

He pulled her from her perch as they slipped down into the water.

Wrenching his sleeved arm up under her head, his lips to hers, warmer, deeper, his free hand roamed under her wet T-shirt forming to her breasts.

Moaning, he touched her soft skin, then down, down as she arched against his hand, moving slowly against him ... then more urgent ... wanting more.

Her hand reaching for him, pulling him free, he tugged at her shorts, freeing her.

The warm water eddied against their bodies, bodies of lovers discovering each other, thrashing but ever mindful of the blue sleeve.

The sleeve blurred as their passions erupted ... flowing over ... streaming through every part of their being.

Chapter 29

Manatee Memorial Hospital

"Dr. Grayson, ER, stat."

"I'm on my way. What's up?" she responded striding down the hall, cell to her ear.

"White male, mid to late thirties, heart erratic, fever, stumbled into the Emergency entrance and passed out. He's in ER one."

Maria rounded the corner, entered the bright operating room and rushed to the side of the man lying on the table. She was not expecting to see her fisherman. Mac was unconscious. "His name is Charles Macintyre. Pull up his record."

An intern quickly had his surgical record on the computer screen. Another intern drew a vial of blood and left for the lab as another called out his blood pressure, reported his temperature was 105. He was trembling with chills.

Mac's eyes fluttered but he couldn't focus. Maria put her hands on his cheeks feeling his feverish skin, forcing him to look at her.

"Mac, what happened?"

"Maria, my arm … my arm … it hurts."

Grayson ripped his shirt from his shoulder revealing dark red lines. His arm was infected and the infection was spreading. She instructed the nurse to cut off the sleeve. His upper arm was red and swollen around the scar.

"Mac, listen to me. When did it begin to hurt? How long has your arm been red?"

"Ah ... ah, several days. Maria, I'm cold ... What's wrong?"

"You have a staph infection. It's spreading. I have to open your wound, check the infection hasn't spread to the bone."

"Am I going to lose my arm?" Mac mumbled.

"Not if I can help it, Captain." Her mind raced with the procedures she had to do to thwart the potential deadly infection.

The anesthesiologist inserted a drip into his arm asking him to count backwards. At ninety-five his eyes closed, his body relaxed, breathing rhythmic.

Maria found the infection was deep compromising his muscle and surrounding tissue. The surgery continued.

Maria adjusted the shades blocking the late afternoon sun. Her patient needed to sleep, needed to remain quiet after his surgery. The infection was bad. It had spread to the tissues wrapped around the muscle. The bone was not infected yet, so she would pump him with antibiotics. How much strength was left? Only time would tell.

Mac opened his eyes. His mind was cloudy. His limbs felt heavy.

Maria was sitting at his bedside holding his hand, her forehead resting on his knuckles.

"You look tired, sweetheart," Mac mumbled, no Bogart inflection in his voice. His words slurred, filled with concern for her. "It's okay. I can take it. I know you tried to patch me up ... again." His lips formed a thin smile in spite of the fog.

Maria lifted her head, looked into his eyes, squeezed his hand. "Oh, Mac, I tried, but the infection ... maybe when we were on the sandbar or, the nurses ... I thought they were being careful but they didn't—"

"No. Not the sandbar. It's my fault." He tried to chuckle but his arm, his head, everything hurt. "I figured out how to change my bandage. I messed up."

"Mac, fishing is everything—"

"Yeah, since I was old enough to hold a stick with a string, a hook holding a worm, dangling over the side of a skiff with my grandfather.

I wanted to be just like him. He told me stories as I sat with him ... dangling my craggy stick. I was a fisherman, Maria." His eyes fluttered. "I was a third generation Macintyre fisherman," he whispered. His eyes closed. He had fallen asleep. She knew he had more to tell her about the boy and his grandfather, but not today.

By morning Mac's mind had cleared, but the need to tell Maria about his life, the life of a fisherman had welled inside. An urgency filled him. He was falling in love with his doctor and if there was any chance she could care for him she had to understand him, the man, the fisherman, not the patient. How could he ever hope she would love him? He had to try.

He felt her enter the room before he saw her. His breakfast was untouched on the tray. Maria smiled as she walked up to his bed, squeezed his hand. "You're awake. How's the arm feel?"

"Hurts, but the nurse just left. Gave me a pill. Maria—" Mac pulled her to him, lifted his head, brushed her lips with his. The stab of pain was worth it as he laid his head back on the pillow.

"Hey, you didn't eat any of your breakfast," Maris said softly her eyes warm responding to his kiss.

"Not hungry. I was waiting to see you. Can you talk ... a little?"

"Yes. How about a cup of coffee. There's enough in this carafe for both of us."

"Yes, please. Maria, I must have fallen asleep yesterday, but I remember I was telling you about my grandfather—"

"You started ... as far as the craggy stick with the hook and your grandfather—"

"He and my pop made a living from fishing. We weren't rich by most standards, not like my Mom's family. Regina was a debutant in New Orleans.

But before she and pop were married they moved with my grandfather to Florida. We lived together in a little house in Cortez, the village where Grandfather came from before going to New Orleans. Everyone said the fishing was better in Louisiana, but Grandfather never believed it, so he was happy to be back in the village where he grew up."

Mac wasn't drinking his coffee. Maria took the cup and filled the glass on the bedside table with ice water, bending the straw to his lips so he could sip to soothe his parched throat. He rested against the pillow, his eyes seeking her violet eyes filled with compassion. A warmth enveloped his body. She had become more than his doctor and he was filled with anguish. He had nothing to offer her. What was he going to do?

Maria felt the pressure of his fingers on her palm as he squeezed her hand. "Sounds like you had a happy childhood."

"It was a great time to grow up. I had aunts and uncles—on Pop's side—who lived in Cortez. Regina made me do my homework after school before I could run down to the dock. The dock was an great place for a kid. Pops was drinking, always remember him drinking, but Regina really loves him. Dotes on him. But the docks, in Cortez, that's where you would find me every chance I got. Maria, it was so exciting," Mac whispered. How could he make her understand, how could he make her feel, want to share his excitement—the docks, the fishermen, the stories?

"You felt like one of them didn't you? Starting as a young boy." Maria's voice was husky. Her eyes warm, trying to understand what he was saying, straining to learn what was in his soul.

"Yes, I guess that's where it started, in the skiff with Grandfather. But when I took over The Regina, Pops was drinking heavily, gambling ... things changed. Tension began seeping through the village, through the fishermen. Then fear."

"Fear? Fear of what?"

"Recreational boaters, sports fishing people. They organized against us, the commercial fishermen. They said that because we used nets we were taking all the fish leaving nothing for them."

"Well?"

"Well what?"

"Did your using nets cause the sportsmen to come up empty?"

"Hell, no. There's plenty of fish for all of us, but they made us look evil, like we were killing Flipper. We tried to fight but fishermen are loners—we want to be left alone, alone in our boats, fishing. So we didn't organize to fight the sport's guys with all their money, their buddies in the government, their cronies who proposed laws banning gill nets. We didn't have a chance. We didn't think it could possibly happen until it was too late. When we realized the impossible was possible we tried to organize with other commercial fishermen ... fishermen from around the state ... but ..."

"But?"

"It was too late. One day ... in 1995 ... we could make a living, pay our bills. The next day what we did for a living was illegal. Gill-net fishing was banned on the west coast of Florida."

"Mac, that was all you knew—fishing. What did you do? The others?"

"People with money drifted in, found Cortez, thought it was beautiful, a nice place to spend a few days fishing ... vacationing. Fishermen are workers. They build their own boats, their own houses. So some of them found part-time work but every chance they got they still fished. The new regulations were stiff. We turned to crabbing, clamming, shrimping, but at every chance we still went out for days trying to catch enough fish with lines.

"The sea, fishing, is in our blood. Many gave up. Now, down at the docks the old codgers are bitter. No more exciting stories. They are beaten down, no light in their eyes. They, the sportsmen didn't have to put us out of business. It was the way it was done. But we can't sit around and say life's over. We had to find other things to do: crabbing, seasonal caste netting, captaining boats. We're adaptable, happy as long as we're on the water."

"But now? What now? Mac, your arm ... I'm not sure if you'll have the strength ..."

"Hey, as long as my arm is attached I'm in business. That's what I'm saying, Maria. I have to adapt ... I will adapt."

Chapter 30

Mac felt the soft touch of a woman's fingers on his hand urging him to wake up. It was almost noon—the lunch tray had been removed, and the tray table pulled to the bottom of his bed.

"Mac, hey, sleepy head."

He was in a deep sleep. *Maria,* he thought opening his eyes.

"There you are. I heard you were back in the hospital. Regular revolving doors. How're you feeling?"

It was Flo, Florence Patterson. Her sleek blond hair framed her face—big blue eyes.

"You look a little peaked. Honestly, Mac, if you don't let that arm heal you're never going to be out on the water again."

"How did you know I was back in the hospital?"

"Ran into Sissy and Shrimp having a sandwich at the Star Fish Market. They're worried about you. I stopped by after your accident but you were out of it. Didn't Studs tell you?"

"No."

"So?" Flo asked pushing a lock of his wavy hair out of his eyes.

"So? What?"

"So, what are you going to do if you can't haul in the big catches?"

"Don't you worry about me. I have all kinds of ideas circling around in this head."

"Yeah? Like what?" her lips puckering.

"Like maybe being the captain of a splashy charter, a sports fishing boat, that's what."

"Oh, Mac, that would be terrific. When new people come into the real estate office, I'll suggest they look you up, go fishing with you, see how wonderful Cortez is. I'll introduce them to you over coffee at the Cortez Kitchen. Or, the reverse, if someone new comes to you first, then you can refer them to me. How does that sound? Personally I think it sounds wonderful. Can we talk about it over dinner? Say, the end of the week? You should be released from here by then. I'll call you." Flo flashed a mega-watt smile plunking her ruby red lips on his mouth in a lingering kiss.

Two interns passed by his door, looked at each other, then back at the blonde with a lip-lock on Dr. Grayson's patient. They were always ready for some juicy gossip. Just wait 'til Dr. Grayson hears about her patient's very friendly visitor.

Chapter 31

*T*he bow of the boat took each wave head on, slamming back into the water only to catch the next wave, slamming again.
Slamming.
Slamming.
Maria closed her eyes, nestled under Mac's chin.
Slamming.
Slamming.
Her thick auburn hair splayed against his shoulder caught in the wind of the forward lurching of the boat.
Slamming.
Slamming,
Loved coursed through her body.
Love filled her being.
Love for her fisherman. Love for Captain Macintyre.
Love—"
"Dr. Grayson."
…
"Dr. Grayson."
Maria raised her eyes to the masked intern facing her across the operating table.
"The patient's under. He's ready."
Maria nodded sweeping Mac's image from her mind.

Bending over her patient, she extended her hand for the scalpel and began emergency surgery on the surfer's leg—torn ligaments from a shark bite.

Chapter 32

Hard Rock Casino, Tampa

The summer heat became intense as July melted into August. Many tourists escaped to the air-conditioned excitement of the Hard Rock Casino, ready to wager what cash was left in their pockets.

The casino rocked.

Slot machines captured gamblers attention with their monotonous, strident pinging. The high-pitched hum filled the air, striking walls painted with swirling blue neon.

Poker tables beckoned to another wave of gamblers. Their laughter mixed with clinking chips, grins, groans, or silence from faces trained to hide emotion—the poker face.

A game of five-card draw poker was in process at a table situated in the middle of a string of tables. Spectators, drinks in hands, stood behind the players two deep.

The game started with six players. After the cards were dealt the first bettor checked. The next, a man called Wiley, the same man Danny Macintyre had beaten a few nights earlier, opened the betting for a $1000. The next three players folded. It was Danny's turn to bet. Beads of sweat formed on Danny's forehead. Pulling a red and green plaid handkerchief from his pants pocket, he swiped it over his brow. "Can't you turn up the air conditioning? It's hotter than hell in here," Danny snapped.

The eyes of the spectators were glued on him: *What was the man going to do?*

"Come on, big boy. Are you going to hold'em or fold'em?" Wiley asked through lips that didn't move. His dark glasses masked the gleam in his eyes as he relaxed against the back of his chair a mere foot around the corner from his opponent. Wiley's dark glasses were targeted like laser beams on Danny, seeking revenge for his big loss, daring Danny to bet.

There were no chips in front of Danny. He had thrown his last chip onto the pile in the center of the table for the ante. He calculated the odds. His hand was a winner. He knew it. Four aces. Wiley would have to have a Royal Flush. Fat chance. Or, a Straight Flush. No way.

Danny picked up his cocktail napkin—Hard Rock Casino printed in red. "My boat. The Regina. Easily worth $10,000." Danny wrote the name of the fishing vessel and underneath signed his name, his personal IOU: Daniel Macintyre. "I call and raise $9,000," he said as he carefully laid the napkin on the top of the chip pile.

"You sure?" Wiley asked his large diamond ring sending shards of light at Danny's chest.

"Of course, I'm sure," Danny hissed.

The player in front of Wiley folded leaving only Danny and Wiley in the pot. Wiley grinned as he called and added nine thousand dollar chips to the pot.

The dealer called for cards and Wiley and Danny both stood pat. When the dealer called for bets Wiley checked and Danny laid down his four aces and a six of clubs face up on the green felt. "How's that Mr. Wiley?"

Wiley grinned. Never taking his dark lens from Danny's face, he laid down his cards—a straight flush.

Danny stared at the cards.

The bastard had won.

Danny's life was over.

Chapter 33

Cortez

Gray sky gave way to light blue, then brilliant orange as the sun breached the horizon. Mac loved this time of day. Waiting for his crew, he leaned against the cabin lulled by the gentle lapping of the incoming tide, sipping a cup of thick black coffee, looking forward to a new day with anticipation—the lure of the sea, the wind in his face dreaming of The Regina pulling away from the dock.

His attention was drawn away from his dream by two husky men dressed in jeans, black T-shirts with sleeves cut away at the shoulder. He watched them as they sauntered down the weathered boards of the dock.

The men stopped alongside The Regina. The bearded man on the right called out, "You the skipper of this boat?"

"I am. What can I do for you?" Mac asked as he threw the dregs of his coffee overboard.

"We're here to take possession," man number two said jumping aboard.

"Whoa. Hold on. You there, stay where you are," Mac shouted at the man who remained standing on the dock but had made a move like he was going to spring after his buddy. "The Regina is my boat. Just what makes you think you can jump aboard and take her?" Mac's face was now inches from number two's face.

"My boss won her last night in a poker game … from a man by the name of Daniel Macintyre. That's what makes me think I can claim her. Now, Mr. whatever your name is, YOU get off my boss's boat."

"Well, Mr. whatever your name is, I suggest you climb back on that dock before I call the Coast Guard, the police, FBI, CIA for starters. Daniel Macintyre doesn't hold title to The Regina. I do, Charles D. Macintyre. Now git," Mac said poking the man in the chest.

Number two man hesitated glaring at Mac, then stepped back up onto the dock. The two men exchanged angry words, turned and strode up the dock, up the stairs to the deck of the Star Fish Market and disappeared around the corner.

Chapter 34

The ambulance siren cut through the sweltering heat as it sped down Manatee Avenue, the EMT relaying the status of the patient to the hospital. "We have a white male, guessing about sixty, in and out of consciousness. BP 44. Badly beaten. Losing blood from a knife wound to the stomach. Cops found him in an ally. We're a block from the hospital."

The van squealed around the corner, down the circular drive, and backed under the portico of the Emergency Entrance. The EMTs transferred the patient strapped to the stretcher off the van onto the rolling gurney and into the hands of the waiting interns.

The beaten man was rolled through the open plate-glass doors, down the wide hall to the operating room, remaining unconscious as he was transferred to the operating table. Dr. Grayson felt his carotid artery under his jaw for a pulse as interns hooked him up to the monitor. The man's face was swollen, bloody, unrecognizable from the beating he had received. She couldn't detect a pulse.

"Crash cart," Grayson shouted.

The man suddenly raised his arms, palms open. "Patty Sue, that you? I'm coming baby. I'm coming." A thin smile twitched over his lips, his eyes wide looking up, staring at the blinding light overhead. "I'm coming."

His arms dropped.

He flat lined, a steady hum emanating from the monitor. Dr. Grayson grasped the paddles. Stepped to the lifeless man.

"Clear." The body jumped.

No response echoed on the monitor display.

"Again," Grayson ordered raising the paddles over the man's chest.

"Clear." The body jerked.

This time the man's heart responded. Grayson began the surgery to repair the wound to his stomach. It was deep and damage to his internal organs appeared extensive. A nurse cleaned the cuts on his face, another bandaged his left hand after checking for broken bones as Grayson continued to operate.

"Do we know who he is?" Grayson asked her gloves and green scrubs bloody, as she took the final stitches closing the wound.

"Wallet in his pocket, Florida driver's license, Daniel Macintyre," a nurse reported.

Dr. Grayson looked down at the patient. *My God, he's Mac's father ... he said the name Patty Sue.* Turning away from the table, she pulled off the white latex gloves and left the cold operating room, discarding the bloody gloves and scrubs into the biohazard hamper.

She'd done all she could but she knew it wasn't enough. Fishing her cell from the pocket of fresh scrubs, she tapped a number.

"Hi, sweetheart," Mac answered, his voice strong, commanding.

"Mac, please come to the Emergency ICU. I'll meet you."

"Maria, are you all right? I'm just pulling away—"

"It's your father. He's dying."

Mac raced down the hall to the ICU, to the third bed locking eyes with Maria, then looked down to the battered man lying on the bed.

"Pops, Pops," he whispered gently grasping the bandaged hand. "I'm here, Pops. It's Mac. Don't you dare check out on me. I need you, Pops." Leaning against the side of the bed, he glanced at Maria as she adjusted the drip.

"I ... I'm sorry, son," Danny whispered. "You'll be fine ... have to believe ... the same blood, Patty Sue's blood, is in you. Her sweetness, passion for life. I failed you."

"No, no, you didn't fail me. Love of the sea, you gave me that, Pops. You're uncanny knowledge of where to go, where to find the fish ... I need you, Pops. Stay with me. We'll get you on your feet again … we'll go out on the water … you, at the helm. Please, Pops, stay with me."

Mac gripped his dad's arm, holding on, clinging to keep him alive.

"Patty Sue … that you?"

"No. It's me, Pops, Mac."

"It's our wedding day, Patty Sue," Danny murmured.

"What? What's the date, Maria?"

"August third."

"Come on, Pops … fight." Mac felt Maria touch his shoulder. He laid his cheek on her hand, closed his eyes, his hand gripping Danny's limp fingers. "Dear, God, wait. Don't take him … we're not done here," he whispered, strangled words through tears escaping closed lids.

A police officer stepped up Maria. In hushed tones he asked when he could speak to her patient. He was on duty when he and his partner found the unconscious man.

"Mr. Macintyre won't be able to answer questions until tomorrow if then. Mac, this is the officer who found your dad."

Mac stood, looked at the officer. "If you want to know who stabbed my dad, go talk to the two thugs who work for Wiley Blackstone. They tried to take my boat. You can probably find Blackstone at the Hard Rock Casino."

Chapter 35

It was almost midnight when Mac shuffled into the dimly-lit hospital chapel. The few pews were unoccupied. He slid into the second row. He didn't know what to do with his hands letting them fall to his side. There had been times out on the water when a sudden storm had threatened his trawler. Fighting the waves he had yelled to God to help him, to help him save his crew. But this was different. No waves buffeting his boat. Now, there were waves of fear that his pops was going to die. He had struggled all his life to see that Mac knew how to watch the sky for a sudden change, a change that could mean danger, a change that meant to head back immediately. And, if there wasn't time, how to point his boat, so he could ride out the storm.

Mac didn't realize until this moment, this moment when he faced life without his mentor, without the man who had given him so much, that he had never asked for anything in return. Mac was too caught up in his own life to see the love in his father's eyes, to see how much his father loved him.

A sudden chill enveloped Mac. He fell to his knees clasping his hands in front of him, looked up at the golden cross through his tears. "Please, please, dear God, give me a chance to tell Pops that I love him. Let him hear my words. I have to tell him how thankful I am that he's my dad. How thankful for all he taught me. He's had a hard life … I could have made it is easier for him … stopped judging him … stopped seeing him through angry eyes cursing as he stumbled in the door. I know he drank to ease the pain, the pain feeling he was a failure."

Mac's head dropped to his steepled fingers.

He caught the familiar scent of her hair as Maria slipped into the pew beside him, kneeling down with him. Her head bowed in silent prayer. He wondered if she was asking for help, or maybe she was asking for a safe journey for Danny. Pops was dead. She had done all she could and now she knelt next to him, their arms touching.

A love so profound warmed his body, dispelling the chill. He gasped. He hadn't been able to look into his father's eyes, hadn't been able to whisper that he loved him.

Maria slid up onto the golden oak pew. She entwined her fingers with Mac's, raised his rough calloused palm to her lips as he slid up to sit beside her.

"Mac … Mac," she whispered.

He turned his tear-stained face to her, his eyes tortured.

"Mac, he's still fighting. I came for you. Let's go sit with him."

They entered the dimly lit hospital room. Mac quickly stepped to his pop's side, laid his hand on his arm, the monitor showed a blip then droned flat.

A sudden chill filled the room. Maria rubbed her arm. Mac stroked his dad's hand.

What was that? Pressure from pop's fingers against Mac's arm?

"Beep … beep … beep."

The monitor registered a pulse. Again. Again. Stronger. Stronger.

Danny's lips curved up ever so slightly, eyes fluttered looking past the woman in scrubs, past his son, inhaling a slight scent of gardenia. The sheet covering his body moved ever so slightly.

"Not yet, Danny. Not yet, my love."

Beep. Beep. Beep.

Mac searched Maria's face. She turned from the monitor, her lips pressed together in a tight line slowly turned into a tentative smile as her head nodded in response. She pulled Mac into a strong embrace, his head leaning into her, his tears staining her green scrubs.

The monitor continued to beep.

It wasn't strong, but it was steady as the chill left the room.

Chapter 36

A woman in a filmy, white-silk shirt tucked into white palazzo slacks tiptoed down the dimly lit hospital corridor to ICU 227. The door of the room was open, the hall lights slicing across the floor. The heart monitor was the only illumination falling over the bed. The man laid in a restless sleep, moaning softly in pain with each breath against the deep wound to his stomach.

The woman stepped to the man, leaned over and softly kissed his lips. Her eyes riveted on him, she picked up his badly swollen hand holding it to her breast. "Danny," she whispered. "I'm here, my love."

Danny's eyes fluttered open. "Patty Sue?"

"Marianne, Danny."

"Marianne?"

"Yes. Remember ... your wedding day ... your friend Marianne. At last I'm here, Danny. Regina is evil. She seduced you on your wedding night. You must leave her. It should have been me, Danny. Your wedding ... I was to be your bride."

"Patty Sue?"

"No, Danny, Marianne. I was always there for you. Helped you with your school work when we were kids, listened to your dreams of becoming a fisherman. You did it, Danny, just as I said you would. I believed in you, not like the Parsons. I love you, Danny, always have, still do ... all these months, years. More than Patty Sue. Way more than Regina."

Marianne stroked his forehead, gently sweeping his hair out of his eyes.

"I'll nurse you back to health. You'll leave the hospital ... come away with me. I have money ... lots of money. We can go travel ... live our golden years together. Oh Danny, this is our chance. I've been planning my escape ... they weren't looking ... I waited until the time was right. A little girl told me where you were ... I've come to you, Danny."

Marianne slithered onto the bed next to him. "My poor darling ... I love you so ... all this time apart." Her hand caressed his cheek, her lips seeking his lips.

"I love you too, Patty Sue."

"No, Danny, Marianne."

"Marianne?"

"Yes, my darling ... your Marianne—"

Suddenly, the sound of footsteps, followed by brilliant overhead lights.

Dr. Grayson entered the room.

"Mother? How did you get in here?"

Marianne, her eyes glazing over, looked down at Danny. "Who are you?" Frightened, her eyes darted around the room. "Where am I?" she screamed. Falling off the bed to the floor, she began to cry as the orderlies Maria had called knelt beside the woman on the floor, gave her a shot, and lifted her into a wheelchair. Mrs. Grayson, sedated, mumbling, was wheeled to the psyche ward.

When Maria called the home, under whose care Marianne Grayson lived, she was informed that they had been searching for her and couldn't understand how she escaped their security system. The chief officer of Sunrise House apologized profusely to Maria adding that an attendant would be dispatched immediately to Manatee Memorial Hospital where she was now, separated from the other patients, under guard, with strict orders not to let her out of his sight.

Chapter 37

Now mid August, Mac had worked hard over the last two months to regain his strength but the arm was still a long way from being whole. Could he do it? Could he take a sports fishing boat out to sea with his damaged arm? He had been struggling with this question for days. And, he was so paranoid about contracting another infection that the blue-sleeve was always with him whenever he was out on the water.

Sitting on the steps to his trailer, watching the wildlife scurry around in the morning dew, birds riding the currents overhead looking for food and twigs for nesting, he decided it was time he did the same—take care of business. Decide what he was going to do with his life. He couldn't hope, couldn't see him and Maria having a life together unless he overcame his injury. The tour boat thing was okay, but it didn't hold the excitement of fighting a big grouper or an amberjack.

"Hell, what are you thinking, Macintyre? You won't be hauling in the fish. But, you sure as hell can take out fishermen who'll pay to find them, pay for the *fun* of reeling them in. And, you sure as hell can feel and be part of their excitement as they're yelling that they've hooked a big one. I'll have Sissy or Shrimp to help me, maybe Studs if he can leave the women alone."

Mac smiled at a pair of squirrels twitching their tails at each other, chirping, performing their mating ritual.

Yup, it was time.

He called the owner he had met with several times regarding his charter boat that was up for sale. It wanted to take her for a trial run. That appointment set, he called Sissy and Shrimp asking them if they would like to go on a little fishing expedition. When they both eagerly agreed he told them where to meet if they could be there in the next thirty minutes.

He threw the dregs of his coffee in a bush and left for the dock.

Within minutes he had parked his truck and was gazing at the lineup of private charter fishing boats moored at a dock a few piers away from the Star Fish Market. There she was—a forty-foot beauty, perfect for up to twenty passengers.

Calypso was outfitted with the latest navigational and fishing equipment, a large cockpit area and a spacious cabin with a restroom. She was built in 1982 and the owner wanted to leave Florida for the mountains of Colorado. The man was done with fishing and had put her on sale at a ridiculous price. Mac would sell The Regina and almost be able to buy the vessel outright.

Adrenalin raced through Mac's veins. The old excitement returned. *Please, dear God, let me do this.*

He strode down the owner's dock to the boat, a smile on his face at seeing Sissy and Shrimp grinning back at him, shuffling from foot to foot. Oh, yeah, his crew was ready for a new adventure.

"Good morning, boys. Did you put the barrel of ice I ordered in the chest?"

"Sure did, Captain. Do you think we can fill'er with fish today?" Shrimp asked, his big black body jumping onto the stern deck after Mac and Sissy.

"We're going to try. I have an idea where the fish are waiting for us, so let's get going. Sissy, you get the bowlines. Shrimp, you cover the stern."

The day had turned out better than Mac could have hoped for but he knew the final test was at the dock. The three wore jeans, T-shirts, and sneakers. A nice benefit of switching from commercial to sports fishing—no heavy rubber boots. Playing it safe, he had securely attached the waterproof blue sleeve over his arm. The wound seemed to have healed nicely but he wasn't taking any chances of getting another staph infection.

Sissy and Shrimp had reeled in seven fish—four grouper, a red snapper, and two amberjacks. They were delirious as one after the other felt a mighty tug on his line.

Heading home Mac let them lie on the deck in the warm sun, a luxury they didn't have before. As serene as it looked, the boat churning the sparkling water, they knew the hard part, the big test for the skipper, was coming up.

They knew that if Mac traded in The Regina and started his own charter business, he would hire a First Mate as his crew—one person and that was it. If he did this thing, he would ask Sissy to be his Mate. Shrimp would be next in line if Sissy couldn't make it. Shrimp was not happy, but he respected Mac's decision. If he made a go of the business, maybe Mac would hire them both. Heck, maybe he'd have a fleet of charter boats and all three would be skippers.

A sports fishing charter usually offered to clean the fish the customer's caught at the dock when they returned for the day. Mac and his crew had discussed how they were going to handle the dockside cleaning. The pier where the Calypso was moored was set up for this service—hoses with fresh water and a high bench for cutting up the fish.

Mac would have trouble cleaning a thirty to forty pound fish, and then the meat had to be cut into chunks and bagged. It was decided Sissy and Shrimp would haul the fish out of the chest hoisting them up on the dock. However, Mac would try, test what he could do.

In the real world, once the chest was empty, Mac would negotiate with the sports fishermen if they wanted to have them cleaned. The fee per pound was set before they left the dock. It was then a matter of whether the fishermen wanted to leave with their day's catch cleaned, bagged and packed into their own ice chests. So, that was how they were going to play it today—a dry run.

Their leisure time over, Sissy and Shrimp rose to their feet and watched as Mac expertly backed into the slip. A smile crossed his face when he saw Maria sitting on the bench waiting for him. She was the only one he had told about testing his strength. They exchanged a wave but she stayed on the bench. It was not a time for celebration. Not yet.

Mac climbed down from the flying bridge as Sissy and Shrimp secured the boat fast to the pilings and then opened the ice chest, heaving the fish up onto the dock. They estimated the seven fish weighed a total of two-hundred pounds—more or less. Sissy pulled the hose from the reel on the dock provided for fishermen to hose down their fish with cold water.

Then it was picture time. Maria was ready as the crew of two loaded their catch in a bright yellow wheelbarrow. A sign, Catch of the Day, had two rows of sharp spikes along the bottom. Mac watched, grinning, as the pair joking over who caught the biggest fish, hung their day's catch on the spikes. Laughing, shoving each other like school boys, they knelt in front of the sign grinning from ear to ear as she took their picture—the scar-faced Asian, and the black man with a scar on his leg.

Twirling around Maria caught Mac's big grin, arms crossed, standing in the boat. If all went well, the picture of the boys would go on a wall—the first catch for the Macintyre and Son, Sports Fishing Charter. Mac waved at her … no, not at her … a blonde standing on the dock throwing him a kiss.

The picture taken, Sissy and Shrimp knocked off their silliness, removed the fish from the spikes reloading them into the wheelbarrow to haul back to the cleaning bench behind the boat. Sissy lifted the big grouper onto the bench, turned to give Mac a hand up onto the dock but Mac wasn't there.

"Where's the skipper," Sissy asked Shrimp.

"He's on the bow fiddling with the line," Shrimp said, his hands on his hips.

"Hey, Mac, come on. We have skinning—"

Mac looked up, slipped, falling backward into the water. The wake of a passing jet ski slammed him into the piling and then he disappeared below the surface.

Boats were tied up on either side so Sissy and Shrimp couldn't jump in after him. They scrambled into the boat, climbed onto the bow and dove into the water. They could see Mac's blue sleeve, then his body, head down.

A sudden chill enveloped Mac. He opened his eyes, began thrashing, gulping for air, choking on water, unable to breathe. He was about fifteen feet away as Sissy and Shrimp swam to him. Sissy pulled Mac's arm around his shoulders holding his head out of the water but Mac's weight with his clothes and fighting for air dragged Sissy down under the water. Sissy fought to the surface. Shrimp circled Mac's waist yelling at him to stop thrashing. Mac blinked feeling a flush of warmth seep through his body.

Two fishermen seeing the attempted rescue jumped in the boat. One grabbed a pole holding it over the side as Sissy, still holding Mac's arm around his shoulder grabbed for the pole and let the man pull them between the moored boats to the dock. The fisherman reached down for Sissy's hand pulling him up on the dock while Shrimp kept hold of Mac who was angrily yelling that he was okay and to let go.

Sissy reached down, grabbed Mac's hand pulling him to safety at the same time Shrimp shoved him up from behind.

Maria watching the rescue, terrified that Mac was going to drown, slumped back onto a bench. It seemed her fisherman was okay as he was thanking the two men who had stopped to give assistance. Then hands on his hips and with a big sigh, he hugged his two crewmen. "Let's get these bad boys cleaned. No more of this foolishness," he said pulling the blue sleeve off, throwing it onto the chest in the stern of the boat, and then stepping to the cleaning bench. With a smile he took the knife from Sissy's hand as they faced each other across the bench.

Mac had practiced on a make-shift bench in the yard behind his trailer. It was time to put the practice into action. He stabilized the fish with his bad arm and used the strength in his right hand to skin and bone the fish handing the remaining fillets to Sissy. Mac threw the carcasses behind him. He would dump them the next day out to sea—dinner for the next one up on the food chain. Sissy rounded the bench to Mac's side and hauled the next fish up to be cleaned and returned to his post, cutting the fillets into chunks, then putting them into plastic bags, and packing the catch into the cooler that Shrimp had retrieved from the truck.

The first two fish seemed tedious to Mac but he soon found a rhythm, and Sissy and Shrimp relaxed, warning Mac—no more tricks. They weren't going swimming again. Tucking the last piece of fish in the cooler, Mac looked up to Maria beckoning her to join them. Striding over the rough boards, she gave him a hug and a big smack on the lips in spite of the fact that he was soaking wet and smelled like dead fish.

"If you three fishermen are finished playing around, I have a bottle of champagne in my car plus big bratwurst hoagies with peppers, onion and garlic," Maria said. "Given your smell, however, I think we better move this little party back to the boat. We wouldn't want anyone to sit downwind of you guys."

"Champagne? You were that sure today's test was going to be successful?" Mac asked.

"Was there ever any doubt, Skipper?" Sissy said punching Mac in the arm, his good arm.

"Not for me," Shrimp said pretending to hit Mac on his bad arm.

The two hightailed it to Maria's car as Mac jumped into the boat, positioned a stool for Maria to step on and steadied her as she climbed down to the deck.

"I thought your dad, maybe even your mom, might come down to the dock to greet you," Maria said.

"I know Pops is up and around but I didn't tell them. You were the only one, other than my two guys," Mac said smiling as he gave her a peck on the lips. "I had to see for myself, see if it felt right, that I could do it."

"And the result, Captain?"

"Other than stupidly falling into the water, I'd say I passed with flying colors," Mac kissed her again, lingering on her pretty lips.

Looking out over the bow, the chill he felt when he was gasping for air and the sudden warmth coursing through his body returned. Shaking off the feeling, he turned to find Sissy trying unsuccessfully to open the champagne.

"Gimme that, you knucklehead." Mac took the bottle and with a surge of strength popped the cork.

Part Three
Chapter 38

Port Orange

A swoosh of warm air was followed by streaks of black and white fur. Peaches and Maggie, after giving a slurp to Liz's cheek and ear, darted out the back screen door Manny was holding open. The pooches chased around the yard happy to be free—Peaches riding shotgun all day with Manny, and Maggie waiting patiently while cooped up in Liz's office, then in the car to pick up a bookcase from a yard sale.

Liz stood at the sink washing dog slobber from her cheeks when Manny came up behind her, circling her in his arms.

"What's my favorite investigator been up to today?" Manny asked nuzzling her neck.

Turning around, Liz beamed. "Nesting."

Manny leaned back, brows arching. "Nice green on your nose."

"Look what I found today—a bookcase ... little shelves. Great yard sale that I passed on my way to work this morning."

"Iced Tea?" Manny asked pulling out the pitcher Liz always kept in the refrigerator when the temperature approached ninety.

"Yes, please. I spent the day making phone calls. Found out some information at the New Orleans hospital Mac told you about. You have any luck?" Liz asked holding the glasses for the tea as Manny poured.

"Yeah. How about we take that bottle of wine in the fridge and drive down to see how much the builders accomplished on our house today? We can sit on our to-be porch and watch the ripples in the river while we swap info."

"Sounds like a plan, partner. But first you have to see my little bookcase. It's perfect to set on the back of a baking table."

"Nice. But last I heard you don't bake. It's either a pizza from the freezer or meals on wheels from the deli."

"Very funny. But look at this." Liz grabbed his hand pulling him out to the cluttered Florida room. The windows were open, fan whirling on high, to dispel the strong paint odor. "There. Isn't it cute?"

"Colorful."

"Oh, yes. Remember we talked about our new kitchen ... Caribbean island colors?"

"I know you like color but all at once? And purple?"

"Not purple, silly. Boysenberry Blast on the outside, Pixie Cup Green inside, and—"

"Ah, Pixie Cup. Matches your nose." Manny kissed the tip of her nose as she tried to wipe away the smudge.

"The shelves are Morning Sun. Won't that start our days off gloriously? Now, for that wine. Let's walk to the house ... give Maggie and Peaches a chance to run off some of that pent-up energy. I'll get the glasses, and oh, and I bought a baguette and some cheese."

"Bought? What happened to the baking?"

"Later, my friend."

The new house was partially framed on a large cement slab facing the Spruce Creek River. Manny's houseboat remained moored at the old, weather-beaten dock, but, while their house was being built, he stayed with Liz during the week. They spent their weekends on his boat. As soon as the house was finished, Liz planned to be carried over the threshold by her dream husband into her dream home.

Sitting against opposite four-by-four posts of the soon-to-be porch, bread and cheese on a towel between them, goblets of wine in hand, the couple clinked glasses and shared a warm kiss. Manny was still in his signature black trousers and black tee, Liz in painting attire—red shorts topped with a blue tee and splotches of Sunny Yellow, Pixie Green, and Purple Boysenberry Blast.

"Tell me what you learned today, Stitch," Manny said, cutting a piece of cheese and passing it to her on a chunk of bread.

Liz smiled. She loved it, when Manny called her Stitch, his pet name for her.

"Well, I managed to find someone, who knew someone, who knew of Maria when she was a resident ... asked all about her, what she was doing etcetera. What I didn't know I adlibbed as any good investigator would have done. In other words I prevaricated to get the information," she giggled.

"And?" Manny said biting into a chunk of bread dipped into a small jar of pesto Liz had tucked into the basket. His eyes closed as he savored the flavors.

"And, this someone, her name is Gladys, looked up the patient record for Arturo Perez—the name Maria gave to Mac who gave it to you. Perez died two years ago. March twenty-third. Cause of death was cardiac arrest. She read me the notes appended to the record."

Liz mimicked Manny's bread dunking into the pesto. "Umm ... so good. Anyway, the report stated that the patient removed his IV. He was found dead by a nurse checking on her patient. It is estimated he had been dead about thirty-five minutes, since that was the nurse's best guess given when she was last in his room. At that time the IV was still working properly and Mr. Perez was alive."

"Thirty-five minutes, huh," Manny said topping off Liz's wine. "A lot can happen in thirty-five minutes. Did the report say anything about the IV machine being turned off? When an IV is removed an alarm sounds unless the button on the machine is switched off."

"Gee, I don't remember her saying anything about an alarm. She read on that they tried to resuscitate him—defibrillator, oxygen, and such, but no luck. His surgeon, a Dr. Young, had visited with Mr. Perez on his regular rounds two hours earlier. No indication he had any visitor other than his doctor. This Dr. Young was the one who raised the issue that he didn't think his patient had died the way it was reported. I asked Gladys to look back on the previous pages—she was reading a computer file. There was a note that Perez had a son, Juan

Perez, who visited him regularly—always in the evening. So, whoever the man was in the striped pants and white doctor's jacket, who Maria said she saw, there is no record of him."

Liz looked out over the thick vegetation to the river. She loved this time in the evening with Manny, talking over their day. This was the first case, she called it a case, that they were working together. Smiling, she sipped her wine as the exhausted dogs flopped down on the cool cement slab. "Your turn, Sherlock."

"Okay. I contacted one of my buddies in Texas. He heads up a team of border guards. I asked him if he knew of a man by the name of Arturo Perez. Honest to God, Stitch, it was like opening the flood gates. My buddy went into a tirade about dueling gang leaders—Perez, State side, and a DelaCruz operating on the Mexican side of the border. Now, get this, the elder DelaCruz passed the leadership of his operation to his son Junior, not a junior like in the second. He's known as Junior. According to my buddy, Junior quickly hired many of Perez's top men, druggies, after Perez died, and, as far as the border guards were concerned, Junior DelaCruz now runs both operations, wrestling most of the Perez business from his son, Juan."

Manny stopped for a sip of wine and a quick kiss. "Love that Pixie Cup Green."

Liz tapped his shoe with her flip-flop, "Go on," she said faking a frown.

"Well, the border guards soon observed that Juan, after he took over the Perez family business, is not the leader his father was. He's weak, and soon after Arturo's death many of the gang members working for the Perez family took up with Junior DelaCruz, who thus snared a bigger share of the drug and gun running businesses."

"Whoa, how about that for a connection, and, Sherlock, either one of the sons, Juan or Junior, could have been the man in stripped pants, which could mean big time danger for Maria. On the other hand maybe Arturo Perez's death has nothing to do with her."

Chapter 39

Anna Maria Island

The evening breeze wafted through the open doors caressing Maria's skin as she swayed in the swing. All in all it had been a good day—no surgeries, a few stitch-and release-patients. Bennett and Donovan flitted in and out of her mind.

Mac's dad was recovering but it would be a while before he was out fishing, or, for that matter, gambling. He'd been released to Regina's care. She had insisted she could do more for him at home rather than staying in the hospital, where he was kept awake with clanging carts and the nurse's infernal stabs for blood samples.

In the twilight, sipping a cup of warm milk, her thoughts lingered over a certain fisherman. She imagined his shadowy boat, a silhouette on the horizon.

The ringing of the telephone cut into her thoughts. Frowning she rose to answer. "Dr. Grayson."

"Dr. Maria Grayson?" the deep, raspy, voice asked.

"Yes."

"I'm calling for an acquaintance of mine. He's learned that a certain lawyer, barrister Ross Bennett contacted you."

"Who are you?" Maria asked, a dart of apprehension shooting through her body.

"It doesn't matter who I am, little lady. What matters is what you *don't* remember, *can't* possibly remember about March twenty-third, so many long months ago that you *can't possibly remember* what happened that day."

"I have no idea what you're talking about, Mr. ... Mr.?"

"Good girl. *No idea.* You just keep saying that and everybody lives happily ever after. On the other hand, *you* might not ... if you make up lies."

A buzz droned in Maria's ear. The call was disconnected.

Maria, her hand shaking, replaced the receiver in the wall cradle. The warm milk forgotten, she poured a glass of wine, picked up her cell on the kitchen counter and tapped Mac's code.

"Hey, this is a pleasant surprise. I thought you might be—"

"Mac, have you heard anything from that private investigator couple you met?"

"Actually, there was a message from Manny on my machine. I just got in. Sissy and I tried a run with a sports fisherman. He caught a beauty."

"The message ... did they find out anything on that man who died ... you know, room 313?"

"Maria, did something happen. Your voice—"

"A man called. Just now. Told me that I *couldn't possibly remember* what happened on March twenty-third. He—"

"Maria, did he threaten you?"

"Sort of. At least I took it as a threat."

"Did you call Bennett or Donovan?"

"No, just you. Mac, Manny's the message. Did he corroborate Donovan's story?"

"He didn't say one way or the other. He just said to return his call as soon as I received his message."

Chapter 40

"Manny, Mac Macintyre here. You left a message to call—"

"Yeah. Liz and I, well, we found out some interesting stuff. First, the information jibes with what the agent told Maria. The man who died in that room that day—cause of death was attributed to cardiac arrest."

"And his name was Arturo Perez?"

"Yes. He headed a drug trafficking operation as well as running guns south over the border to Mexico."

"Okay, same as what Donovan told us. Maria just called. Some weirdo threatened her. I know he scared her. She said the caller told her to keep her mouth shut. That she didn't *see* anything and to keep it that way."

"Oh, oh. Not good. Sounds like someone is getting worried. But, Mac, I have more. I checked with one of my buddies. He was a border agent at that time. Still is. He said when Perez died, another guy stepped right in. They think his name is DelaCruz. Took over the operation. My friend said they haven't been able to get close to the character. They did nab one of his henchmen. Squealed like a prairie dog caught in a trap. Coughed up his leader's name. Don't laugh—"

"I'm not laughing, Manny. What's his name?"

"He goes by Junior."

"That doesn't jibe, as you say, with dangerous," Mac said rubbing his arm.

"These guys mean business, Mac. Maybe Maria should take up that lawyer's suggestion. Think about telling the feds what she saw and ask for protective custody."

"She says she didn't see anything. She won't do it, Manny. Won't leave the hospital, all she's worked for. She's not going to buckle under threats when she didn't see anything. Unless—"

"Unless what?"

"Well, maybe it was so bad she's block it out."

"Let me do some more digging," Manny said. "I don't suppose the caller gave his name?"

"I doubt it. She would have said."

"Stitch and I have been talking and we've decided to take a run to Anna Maria Island. We both think that Maria could be in danger. These drug guys get rid of anything or anyone who gets in their way."

"I agree. I'll call her back, tell her what you found out … about this Junior DelaCruz."

Chapter 41

One pot of coffee at 6 a.m. and now a second was gurgling—8 a.m. *A robot. Thank God*, Maria thought. *I'm a robot performing my morning routine, the same routine I've performed every morning, every day for decades. Otherwise, I'd curl up on the swing and never move.*

Hands on hips, she paced from the front door to the outdoor dining area and back. The quick movement of her feet released the tension building in her body, while her mind sifted through everything that had happened to her in the last few months.

Finding her mom in Danny's room, lying next to him in his hospital bed, had been frightening. Since then, Marianne Grayson had turned belligerent, insisted on staying with her lover never acknowledging Maria as her daughter. She called the woman in the white coat a devil, and then called her Patty Sue, screaming she would never let her marry her Danny.

Then there was the phone call. Maria kept pacing, going over and over the words the man uttered, his threat. Did she misunderstand what he said? No. She had been threatened. And then there was Manny's call to Mac—Arturo Perez. Of course, she already knew the name, but hearing the name again gave credence to Donovan's warning, his warning that she was in danger. And, now a new name, DelaCruz.

She had to do something to protect herself. *The gun in my nightstand. I'll feel safer if I have it with me,* she thought. Grabbing her bag off the dining room table, she marched into the bedroom, retrieved her revolver, tucking it inside the pocket of her shoulder bag. That piece of business done, she returned to the kitchen. Poured another cup of coffee.

Looking at the swing's gentle sway, a balmy breeze entering the house through the open French doors, she ambled over, sat down, tapped her foot on the mosaic tile. This time the sway of the swing did not soothe her. She sat stiffly. *What else?*

Her cell rang—an unfamiliar ring tone and an unfamiliar caller ID: MRH.

Maria took a deep breath. "Hello," she whispered, fear rising to her throat. Who was it?

"Dr. Maria Grayson?"

"Yes. Who's this?"

"My name is Mrs. Connors. I'm the Director of Human Resources at Montgomery Regional Hospital."

"I'm sorry, but I haven't heard of your hospital. Where are you located?"

"Juneau, Alaska."

"Good heavens, I'm in Florida. You must have the wrong—"

"I know, Dr. Grayson, but your name was sent to us by the Medical Department of Tulane University, New Orleans. We are conducting a search for two surgeons. This is an exploratory call, Dr. Grayson. I know it must seem to you that Alaska is terribly far away, to say nothing of the different climate." Mrs. Connors paused, chuckling. "I'm sending you a packet of information, but before it arrives I wanted to make contact. You come so highly recommended that we are taking the unusual step of sending you information on the positions we are looking to fill, hoping you will not decline out of hand. We are in a great need of a young surgeon, a surgeon who will take up residency in our beautiful state."

"Can you say who recommended me?"

"Yes. A Dr. Benjamin Webber. He said you might be ready to leave Florida. I do hope that's the case. I look forward to hearing from you."

Maria said goodbye as a chill ran up her spine. *Why would Dr. Webber, Ben, my ex-husband recommend me? Was he the one who threatened me? The voice was muffled, like he was speaking through a piece of flannel. It could have been him.*

Chapter 42

Torrential rain swamped the Tampa Bay area. Cars pulled to the shoulder of the roads. Anyone outside ducked for cover. Ten minutes later the sun was peeking through the clouds—a typical storm spasm in Florida. The cars continued on their way and people went about their business. One last gust of wind sent any lingering clouds east.

Maria was running late. Backing out of her garage, she gunned the engine and headed to the Manatee Bridge. Her mind was a jumble, going back to her mother. The incident was unsettling. But, when she called Sunset House after her mother was returned, she sounded as if she recognized Maria's voice.

Maria had tried a long shot. She swore she heard her mother gasp when she heard the name Arturo Perez. But why? Then there was that conversation not an hour ago with Mrs. Connors at the Montgomery Regional Hospital, in Alaska of all places. *Well, if I want to get away from more threats, Alaska might not be a bad place to go, but not if my ex-husband recommended me. I'm being silly. That man who called didn't sound at all like Ben. But, the voice was muffled.*

Squinting, she glanced at the car's clock. She was really late her for her shift in the ER. Her foot responded pushing the gas pedal down. Turning onto the bridge to Bradenton, the sun smacked her in the eyes.

All of a sudden her car lurched. Someone struck her on the left side, sending her car spinning, into the guardrail. Hitting her head

Maria gripped the wheel. Stomped on the brake, shut her eyes bracing herself, she mercifully blacked out. She was going to plunge off the bridge into the deep river below.

There was a knock … a soft knock on the window. Maria's eyes fluttered in response. Slowly opening her eyes she looked through the steering wheel, through the windshield at a man … a police officer. Her car had not fallen from the bridge.

Everything seemed far away … in a fog … in slow motion.

A horn … blaring … it was coming from her car. The keys were swinging leisurely in the ignition. Her right hand reached out … turned the key. The engine stopped releasing the door locks.

The officer opened the car door. "Are you all right, ma'am?"

"I … I think so. My car … am I going to fall off the bridge?"

"No. But it was close. Take my hand. I'll help you out."

Grasping the officer's hand, Maria slid her legs around the seat, but her legs were spongy, surely they would buckle if she tried to stand.

"Give me a minute … still shaky."

The officer called to his partner sitting in the squad car running Maria's license plate, asking him to bring over a bottle of water.

Nodding, the officer came over to Maria. "Here, ma'am, drink this. What's your name?"

"Maria Grayson. Dr. Maria Grayson. Where's the other car? The one that hit me?"

The officer looked down the bridge. "He didn't stop. From the looks of the dent on your left side, it was a black car. The way he hit … he shoved you into the guardrail. Your car took out a piece of the rail. Stopped short of going off the bridge. He had to have known he hit you. Were you stopped on the bridge?"

"No. If anything I was going too fast. I'm late."

"A description of the car—we know it was black. Make? Man or a woman driving? See anything?"

"No, it happened so fast. The sun was in my eyes." Maria turned, fished in her tote for her cell and placed a call to the hospital, telling them she had been in an accident. She'd call as soon as she knew when they could expect her.

Her body had stopped shaking so she slid the rest of the way out of the car. "Thanks for the water. I can stand now." She shook her head when the officer put his hand on her elbow to steady her. "I'm okay."

She looked at the side of her car then up at the officer.

"Okay if I call for a tow?"

"I already have, ma'am. My partner and I sent for a backup team to process the scene, take your statement, then we can take you to the hospital."

The second squad car arrived. The officers took pictures, took measurements, and took down her statement. Maria called Mac telling him what happened. He told her to stay put, he'd pick her up on the bridge in fifteen minutes. Take her home, to the hospital, or to a car rental agency—whatever she wanted.

Maria stared at the damage to her car. *Was it an accident? Oh, God, was someone trying to kill me?*

Chapter 43

Hearing the distress in Mac's voice, as he related the facts that Maria's car was almost forced off the Manatee Bridge, Manny reassured him that he and Liz would leave for Anna Maria Island immediately—estimated time of arrival about five o'clock.

Traveling west on I-4, Liz called Maria. "Hey, girl friend, I'm Liz Stitchway, Manny's to-be wife. What the heck are you doing trying to drive off a bridge instead of over it?"

"Liz, it was scary. I thought for sure I was going through the guardrail."

"Mac just called Manny, and for you to know, we are on the road as we speak. Manny is going to drop me off at the hospital … are you at the hospital?"

"Yes. I finally finished with the police at the scene of the accident … so many questions. My car has been towed to the repair shop and I have a rental."

"Good. Manny is going to meet with Mac. Check if the police have any leads on the car that hit you. Meanwhile, you and I can have a glass of wine, a little down time. I want to hear all the details of your accident."

"Oh, Liz, I'd like that … just what the doctor ordered … some girl talk. We'll go to my house on the beach."

"By any chance is your beach house near the Sandbar restaurant."

"Practically next door."

"Do you mind if we walk down the beach to the Sandbar? I'd like to look at their menu for our wedding reception. You're not the only one with the jitters, I have them too—wedding jitters."

Closing her phone, Liz looked at Manny who had lifted her hand to his lips.

"What?" Liz asked with a grin.

"Wedding jitters?"

"Just girl talk."

After a hot shower and a change of clothes Maria began to relax. She was enjoying her vivacious new friend. She thought Liz was probably a very effective investigator as she could disarm anybody into giving her information.

They strolled to the Sandbar, to one of the outside tables sheltered from the sun's late afternoon rays. Ordering a glass of white wine, they leaned back in their chairs. Maria closed her eyes, letting the music of the waves rippling ashore wash over her body.

"Oh my. Oh, my."

Liz giggled. "Crystal. Hello. I'd like you to meet my—"

Maria smiled and nodded to the woman in the floppy hat decorated with bright tomato red hibiscus blooms. The smiled faded as the woman appeared to be distressed, staring at her as she plopped on the chair next to Liz, her hands clutching the edge of the table.

"Elizabeth, I'm sorry to interrupt … normally don't intrude … but when I saw you—"

"Crystal, I'd like you to meet Dr. Maria Grayson. She had a scary experience—"

"Yes … your car … you're in danger, Dr. Grayson."

Maria smiled. "Yes, it was a very scary accident as Liz said. That's why she suggested we have a glass of wine. She's trying to settle my nerves, but how did you know—"

"It wasn't an accident. A man is hunting … found you … hit your car to kill you."

Maria's hand pressed against her heart trying to stop the pounding. "I … I…"

"Crystal, are you sure? Can you see him? Who is he?" Liz asked her hand reaching for Maria's arm to steady her. "Crystal is a psychic, Maria. She senses things."

Crystal gently touched Maria's shoulder, stared into her eyes. "The man ... no ... there are men after you ... a medal, gold—"

"Crystal, it's been a very trying day for Maria. Perhaps it would be better if we came to see you ... at your home. Can we call you later?" Liz asked.

Crystal tore her eyes from Maria, slowly turned her head to Liz, her hand falling into her lap. "Yes ... yes, of course. Call ... later. I'm sorry to barge in on you and your friend." Crystal's chest rose and fell in a slow rhythm and, without looking at Maria, pulled herself up off the chair, turned away, her hat shading her from the heat, muttering as she made her way down the beach disappearing through a break in the bushes.

"Well, that went well ... not. Let's order," Liz said watching Crystal ducking out of sight and signaling the waitress for two more glasses of wine and menus.

Maria sighed, stared out at the water.

"Yoo-hoo. Me to you. Come back ... the accident?"

Maria turned back to Liz. "I want to see her again. Maybe she can help me."

"Okay, but I haven't really tested her, you know, like testing something she predicted—did it come true. I do know she scared us to death the night I met Mac and his mother."

Conversation went on hold, as Liz ran her finger down the menu, pointed to an entree and handed the menu back to the waitress. Maria nodded to bring her the same.

"Maybe she has it all wrong," Liz said sipping her wine.

"Wrong?" Maria asked, again staring out at the waves.

"Yeah. Maybe it's Mac who's in danger ... being a fisherman. Manny says it's more dangerous than being a cop, after all he had that fishing accident. But I guess that turned out well—he met you." Liz smiled, sighed. Maria didn't seem to be listening.

"As I said, Maybe it's Mac. Crystal got all worked up when she saw Regina and now you."

"Worked up ... how?"

"Oh, boy. Really crazy. There was this knife thing—"

"Knife? Liz, what are you talking about?"

"Disappearing knife that had Regina's karma on it, windows flying open, curtains blowing. Aunt Jane's cat hissing … poor thing nearly had a stroke. The cat, not Aunt Jane."

"Liz, I had a job offer."

"Job? Promotion?"

"Yes, but not here … in Alaska."

"My God, Maria, you can't go to Alaska. Mac—"

"Mac may have another lady friend. I've heard about, seen a blonde."

"Oh now, girl friend, from what Manny tells me, you are the only one for that big fisherman, and Maria, he really is a hunk."

Maria smiled at Liz calling Mac a hunk, because that was her first impression when she saw him lying on the operating table, even with all the loss of blood. "But, maybe I'm bringing him bad luck. Maybe I'm the one, as you just said, putting him in danger, and maybe I'm moving too fast. Maybe I should look elsewhere."

Chapter 44

Studs lit the reefer and, settled back in the tattered recliner. His new buddy was supplying him with cheap marijuana and had asked nothing of him for this latest little packet. *Maybe I should step up the game,* he thought relaxing, looking around at the shabby room he rented near the docks. *Mac's never going to do any big fishing again, not with that gimpy arm. I have to move on. There's more where this came from.* A calm flowed through his veins as he inhaled deeply, held it, then exhaled, feeling his cell vibrating in his pocket.

"Hello."

"I was told you know Dr. Maria Grayson. Is that true?" The voice was muffled, as if talking through a mask. Man? Woman? He couldn't tell.

"Yeah, sure. Who are you? Wally, is that you?"

"Whoever. I have a business proposition for you. If you accept, you will receive a letter ... an envelope, day after tomorrow. The envelope will hold a retainer, $5,000 for our business arrangement. Should I go on?"

"Yeah, sure. *What's this, some kind of test? Wally seeing if I'll step up to bat ... or cross him?* Studs inhaled, slowly releasing the narcotic in his throat. "What's the deal?"

"You must take Dr. Maria Grayson away. Far away. She must NEVER return."

"Whoa, and just how I am I supposed to convince the lovely doctor to leave?"

"That's up to you … maybe a little excursion on a boat … out to meet the fisherman … yes, out fishing. Rent a boat. Go to Key West, the Pelican Inn. A room will be reserved in your name. You will arrive alone. If you arrive alone, you will be paid handsomely."

"So, somehow Grayson doesn't arrive with me?"

"You said it. I didn't. If you arrive without the *lovely doctor* you will be paid. However, you must send proof that Grayson is indeed gone … send the proof to a PO Box in Orlando, and, in return, you will receive a package … $30,000."

"Like what kind of proof? What will satisfy this little business arrangement?"

"She wears a distinctive cross on a chain around her neck. There's a small ruby in the center. Send that cross to me and you will receive payment in return."

"Okay, we have a deal. When is this business arrangement to take place?"

"Within the next two weeks. I will know if you keep the retainer without fulfilling your end of the bargain. In which case, I will make sure the authorities have proof of your latest drug package. Do we understand each other?"

"Understood."

Chapter 45

It was definite. Well, not quite definite. The test was a success but Mac and the owner of Calypso hadn't come to terms yet. Mac had to have The Regina appraised, but before he made arrangements for an appraisal, he had to clean her up—scrub her down, then paint. She really needed a paint job. He wasn't sure a deal was even possible financially. If not, then what was he going to do? Captain somebody else's boat for pay? The thought made his stomach roil.

Never!

He'd just have to keep The Regina.

Two suited men were waiting at The Regina as Mac strode down the dock to tell his crew what he planned for them today. The men weren't smiling and they certainly weren't dressed to go fishing. Their demeanor seemed sour to Mac.

The tallest of the men stepped forward as Mac approached him.

"Daniel Macintyre?"

"Charles Daniel Macintyre. What can I do for you?"

The man flashed a badge. "We represent the Central Florida Regional Bank. We're impounding your boat, The Regina. The bank holds the loan and a Mr. Wiley Blackstone says he's the owner and wants his boat. He's suing unless the bank hands over the title."

"I told his two goons that my dad no longer owns The Regina. I do."

"Well, Macintyre, Wiley has a note," he laughed looking at his partner, "written on a Hard Rock Casino napkin. It seems your dad put up The Regina in a poker bet. Lost the bet and we're here to deliver the boat to the winner."

"Well, Daniel Macintyre is not the owner. I am and I have the title to prove it. So get out of my way."

Mac brushed by the man but his partner stepped in front of him, barring him from boarding The Regina. "Okay, Macintyre, we'll give you a week. Settle the title issue with the bank and Mr. Wiley. If not, we'll be back."

Mac stood on the dock, a puff of air whistled out over his teeth as he watched the men saunter up the dock. As he squinted he saw Maria marching in his direction, passing the two men without so much as a glance. They turned to look at the pretty lady, made a remark and continued walking. Maria didn't slow her stride in his direction, arms at her side, fists clenched.

He knew she was mad at him and he knew why. When he made his customary call the night before to see how her day had gone, she didn't answer. It had happened before—her being delayed at the hospital, not answering his call. Last night he had given her time, then called again. With no answer he called the hospital. There had been a bus accident on I-75. Several patients had been transported to Manatee Memorial Hospital, a trauma center. When Mac asked if Dr. Grayson was there, the woman at the nurse's station told him she had been operating but had left an hour ago.

Mac called her home again and left a third message to call him. He tried her cell phone several times and the hospital again, but didn't leave any more messages.

Maria finally answered her cell, informing Mac that she was on her way home when she was flagged down by a police officer. Apparently, the hospital's security department had become alarmed at his calls and had alerted the police that she was missing.

"I'll talk to you in the morning," she said slamming the phone down ending their conversation.

Mac watched her approach. *Well, it's morning. If it's a fight the lady wants ...* "then bring it on," he mumbled.

Sissy and Shrimp were on the boat scrubbing every surface in preparation for the next step—painting. They looked at Maria then at Mac. Both were stone-faced. Mac stood on the dock feet wide apart, arms crossed.

"Don't you ever again tell Hospital Security that you can't find me," Maria spit out within a foot of his face.

"I was worried. You should have been home. And, I didn't talk to Security."

"Oh, no? Well you scared everyone into thinking I had been kidnapped. My schedule is my business. I have emergencies to tend to. People's lives are at stake. You just have to wait your turn."

"Wait my turn! So that's how it is. Well, I'm done waiting for my turn. Thanks for fixing my arm. It's healed and I'm moving on. You just go on back and save people's lives. There's no place for you here."

"I couldn't agree more. I'm used to being on my own and not having someone questioning my every move." Maria turned and marched back where she came from. Mac didn't watch her leave. He was already on the boat placing a call to the boat shop, ordering the paint he needed. Sissy and Shrimp, heads down, scrubbed the deck to the bare wood.

Chapter 46

The black SUV pulled into the driveway of the beach house. Manny turned the key in the ignition gazing out the windshield. "Quite a house. Sure you have the right address?"

"Sure, I'm sure, Sherlock. I've been here before. It's no different than those people up north who call their mansions a summer cottage." Liz giggled. "We look like a couple of ghouls in our black shirts and slacks. When we get to Crystal's she's liable to freak out."

Maria, head down, stepped down the stairs.

"Oh, oh. She looks grim," Liz said. "Something's wrong."

"Probably wondering what you got her into," Manny said getting out to open the door for Maria.

"Me? She's the one who … Hi, Maria."

Maria nodded, got in the backseat, and Manny drove the women in silence to their meeting with Crystal. He glanced once at Stitch, flicked his eyebrows, then back to the road. First time he'd been with two women who said nothing.

A young girl greeted them at the door with a slight wave to enter and to follow her. She stepped aside, again with a slight movement of her hand signaling them to join Crystal.

Crystal sat at the small round table both palms open, beckoning them to her. The shades were drawn. Numerous white candles had been placed around the room, their flames flickering in the slow rotation of the ceiling fan. A small pad of lined paper, a pen placed on top, laid in the center of the table. The room looked the same as it had at their last visit, with the exception that Maria sat in Jane's spot.

Liz took note of Crystal's floppy straw hat perched on a peg at the top of the coat tree in the corner. Today it was ringed with white daisies, a nice touch if Crystal chose to go out in the white muumuu she was wearing, sprinkled with large black leaves.

Settled in their chairs, Crystal smiled looking into their eyes, one after the other, pausing on each face.

Manny broke the silence. "When Liz set up this meeting, I believe she mentioned that we were bringing pictures," he said pulling a photo of the seventy-one-year-old Camacho DelaCruz from his breast pocket laying it in front of Crystal. The picture his border patrol buddy had sent to him.

Crystal's eyes narrowed as she pulled the picture a skosh toward her with her right index finger.

Liz unfolded a newspaper clipping of Arturo Perez, pressed it flat with her palm and set it on the table next to Camacho DelaCruz.

"Did you bring the letter?" she asked with a piercing look at Liz.

Manny looked at Liz, shrugged his shoulders. Liz shook her head.

Crystal dismissed their answer fastening her eyes on the clipping, drawing it closer, next to the photo Manny had presented. "No good. I can't see the eyes clearly," she said waving her fingers over the clipping. Tearing a sheet from the tablet, she pushed it in front of Liz. "Write the man's name."

Liz picked up the pen and wrote Arturo Perez on the sheet then slid the paper back to Crystal.

Crystal, the outstretched fingers of her right hand held tight together, rapidly traced over the name several times. Her body did not move, only her eyes, her lids rising sharply. She stared at Maria. Maria did not move in response, staring back at Crystal.

The psychic continued to hold Maria with her eyes. "You are in grave danger, my dear. There are men, bad men, one all white, after you. I see no escape."

Liz squirmed in her chair. "Crystal, are the men ... the bad men ... the ones you see in the picture?"

"More. Many more. There's a letter ... no, a charm," she said continuing to stare at Maria.

Maria's breath was coming in short gasps, her fingers fumbling for the cross from under her white T-shirt, her eyes remaining locked with Crystal's.

"No, no. Not that."

Maria reached into the left pocket of her black capris. She placed the picture of Mac she had taken on their excursion to the sandbar. His Saint Christopher medal hung down on a gold chain onto his bare chest.

"Yes. He's one of them. Give me the other picture you have … your other pocket."

"But how …" Maria did as Crystal asked. She removed the picture from her right pocket, the copy of the picture the attendant had sent from her mother's dresser, the picture of Patty Sue in her wedding dress standing with Regina, Mrs. Parsons and Maria's mother, Marianne.

Crystal snatched the picture from Maria's hand, held it to her breast. Tears began running down her cheek, breaking into quiet sobs. The picture dropped on the table.

The young girl who had greeted the guests earlier ran into the room. "Grandmother, come with me." She put her arms around Crystal's shoulders, helping her to her feet. "You must lie down. I'm sorry," she said looking at Manny, "but you must leave. She hasn't been herself this week. Her heart … call back … another day."

As Crystal's granddaughter led her from the room, Manny, Liz, and Maria picked up their pictures and left. Liz grasped Maria's hand as they walked to the car. The doctor was visibly shaken.

Chapter 47

"Manny, you awake?" Liz asked nudging his shoulder. "Manny, Manny?' she whispered in his ear, her lips touching his lobe.

"Umm." Manny rolled over pulling her against him. "Morning already?"

"That was exciting yesterday wasn't it? I mean Crystal and all. I think she's really psychic. What do you think?"

"I think I'd like a few more minutes of sleep. We discussed this, the Crystal thing, last night."

Liz rolled on her back. "Maria didn't seem fazed … well, maybe a little … right after we left. I mean the whole bad men being after her thing. She never really said a word did she?"

"She said goodbye." Manny sat up rubbing his eyes checking the clock. "Look at the time. It's almost seven. I told Mac I'd meet him at the dock. He's painting his boat. Getting ready to sell it …

His words trailed off as he turned on the shower.

The Regina was in dry dock perched on scaffolding, her hull sanded, primed, ready to be painted. Manny snapped a picture of her with his cell phone and sent it to Liz with the caption, "Wish you were here. Yes, I wore my old jeans."

He strolled up to Mac, juggling a cardboard tray with six notches all but one holding a takeout coffee.

"Look at that, Shrimp. A man with a heart. Obviously cares about us slave laborers. Not like someone else we know," Sissy said grinning at Mac.

"Okay, I get the message. Take a coffee break and then let's get this baby painted. A nice hot day like this, and a couple more in the forecast, we can get her back in the water, the sooner the better—show her off."

Sissy and Shrimp plucked their coffee from the tray and ambled over to the dock to sit, dangling their feet off the edge.

"Thanks for the coffee, Manny," Mac said leaning against the scaffolding.

"Where's your other guy? I have a coffee for him."

"Didn't show. I think he sees the handwriting on the wall—Sissy and Shrimp will alternate as my first mate if I go ahead ... sell or trade The Regina for a charter boat. I think Studs is looking for a job, but he could have picked up a couple extra bucks helping with the painting. I hope he's not just *looking* at women." Mac chuckled. "How did it go with the psychic yesterday? Anything startling?"

Manny thought a moment. He wasn't sure what to say. "It was kinda loony, Mac. We each—me, Liz and Maria—had a picture in our pocket ... just to see if Crystal said anything *startling* as you say."

"Did she?"

"Mainly rambled on about bad men being after Maria and that she was in danger."

"Was Maria, okay?"

"She didn't react much ... said goodbye ... Liz and I dropped her at home and then went on our merry way. Maria didn't seem to want to hang out with us ... tired, I guess."

"Okay, skipper. You and your friend going to stand around all day or are we going to slap on the rest of the paint?" Sissy asked as he and Shrimp shuffled up to Mac, and then moved on picking up their brushes continuing to paint where they had left off.

Mac smiled at his crew, downed the last drop of his coffee tossing the empty cup into the trash barrel.

"Where do you want me?" Manny asked.

"My boys and I have the hull under control but we didn't get to the wheelhouse, inside the cabinets. Pops shoved snacks and stuff on a few of the shelves. If you could clean it out and paint inside ... anyplace else you see that needs it would be great."

Manny climbed up the scaffolding and boarded the boat, a trash bucket holding a gallon of white paint and a brush in hand. He looked out the windows, around the cabin, at the water slapping the dock's pilings. *Not a bad way to spend the day, out on the water fishing,* he mused. Setting the paint and brush to the side, he squatted in front of the first cabinet, pulled the trash can to his side and started to empty the cabinet. Mac was right, it was messy—candy wrappers, a couple of empty beer bottles and a half-full bottle of scotch. The top shelf of the next cabinet was crammed full of papers. "You know there are unopened envelopes in here. Looks like some bills and ... look at this." Manny, holding up an envelope, yelled over the side at Mac. "The return address: Arturo Perez, and underneath, Claude Steinham, Lawyer. It's addressed to Daniel Macintyre--postmarked over two years ago ... almost three."

"That's my pops. He must have stuffed it in the cabinet. Perez. That's the name of the man whose death Maria seems to be mixed up with. Open it."

Manny climbed down the scaffolding, slit the flap and pulled out a handwritten letter on yellowed white paper. He looked at Mac painting a few feet away, back at the letter and began reading out loud.

>   *To: Daniel Macintyre*
>
>   *Today my doctor found a tumor in my brain. I'm scheduled for surgery next week. The doctor says my chances for survival are good, but I have a different take and believe my days are numbered with or without the surgery.*
>
>   *When I finish with what I have to say to you I will give this letter to my lawyer in a sealed envelope. He will not know what it contains. His instructions are that upon my death he is to mail this to you as I have addressed.*
>
>   *I cannot leave this life until I confess something I did thirty or so years ago.*
>
>   *I was a young punk in my family business—our own kind of pharmacy. I know, I know, it was bad but family is family. My father was a big deal and he made me learn the business from the ground up. I met Patty Sue Parsons six months before she was going to marry you. Her mother and father, particularly*

her father, were against you marrying their daughter and were making life for her unbearable.

It was suggested by another, that Patty Sue was a nervous wreck and needed help. I was to bump into her at a bar that night where she would be waiting for her fiancé. She was told to arrive early and that a friend was going to help her calm down, even enjoy the remaining few months until her wedding.

We met. She was very nervous. Scared. Her father had made an ultimatum that he would ruin you if she went ahead with the upcoming nuptials.

I told her I had something that would calm her. We went out the back door into the alley and I gave her a packet of powder—pure coke—and told her to sniff it. Her nerves calmed almost instantly. It was unusual to have such an immediate effect. She was very susceptible to the drug.

After that, we met several times a week and it was on these subsequent visits that I saw just how susceptible to the drug she was. There was never an issue of payment. As you know, with the Parsons, money was no object. They doted on their two daughters, Patty Sue and Regina, giving them everything imaginable.

Three days before the wedding I had a call from the person who led me to Patty Sue in the first place. Said Patty Sue was in desperate need of my help.

I was told where to find her, at the beach house, and I immediately went to her. She had called as well so I knew she was in a bad way. We walked down the beach. This time I used a needle. Patty Sue continued to tremble. Asked for more. And more. Stumbling, I took her to my car where she collapsed and died.

She is buried on our property, a large horse farm in Ocala, Florida, the Perez ranch. You will find her remains about a quarter mile north from the main barn, a dirt road. She's in the center of a cluster of three lemon trees if you should wish to go there. However, I'm not sure my son Juan will allow you on the property. Perhaps he will if you show him this letter.

I have never told anyone about Patty Sue, that she had died of an overdose. I let the gossip build—Patty Sue was a runaway bride.

Why am I telling you this? To give you some peace and to tell you her dying words were that that she loved you very much.

Daniel, Patty Sue would never have left you at the altar.

Arturo Perez

Chapter 48

Cortez

The twenty-seven foot Sun Rae sped south over the calm Gulf waters. The sun was reaching its apex in the brilliant blue sky, dotted with tufts of white cotton mixed with gray clouds way off on the horizon.

Maria leaned back in the lounger on the aft deck, the wind from the cruiser blowing cool air over her body. Her lush auburn hair anchored in a ponytail under a Tampa Bay Buccaneers ball cap kept the sun out of her eyes. *No wonder Mac loved fishing every day, loved the Gulf waters feeding his bank account as well as his love for the sea.*

She had to see him.

Their fight was horrible, both saying things they didn't mean or did they? That's what she had to find out. When Studs called, telling her Mac wanted to see her, asking Studs to bring her to him, she had readily agreed.

Now out on the water, a beautiful day much like the day Mac had asked her to accompany him—testing his idea for becoming a tour-boat captain …going out on a picnic … going out to the sandbar to look for seashells … going out to the sandbar where he made love to her, where she made love to him.

Studs said Mac wanted to enjoy today with her, and her with him, to relax away from threatening phone calls, from someone trying to run her off the road. Mac felt a few hours out to sea was just what the doctor needed ... peace. The tranquility of the sea ... with him.

"Studs, how long until we meet up with Mac? I didn't know he was going out today?" *How would I, we haven't spoken to each other since the fight,* she thought.

"At least an hour. It was a spur of the moment thing. Make yourself comfortable, sweetheart."

Sweetheart. That's a funny thing for him to say. But then he's known for his way with women. But I'm not just any woman. As far as Studs is concerned, I'm Mac's woman.

Maria closed her eyes, her full lips drawing into a smile. *Mac was so thoughtful. What was it that Studs said? Oh, yes, Mac wanted her to experience the tranquility of the sea. Tranquility. Lovely word.*

Suddenly restless, she was anxious to see Mac, talk, figure out where they were going in life, what they each wanted, needed for themselves. What did they expect from each other? Could she give him what he desired, and could he be the partner she had not dared to dream of having? Until she met him, she had no desire to be with a man, let alone a relationship. Were they in a relationship or not? Was there someone else—a blonde?

Joining Studs she sat next to him, his hands grasping the wheel, eyes straight ahead, the windshield protecting them from the stiff breeze. "This is a nice boat, Studs. Sleek. Fast. You rent it?"

"Yup, with an option to buy. Maiden voyage. There's a bottle of wine in the refrigerator. Would you pour us a glass?"

"All right." *My, my, looking to buy this little beauty. I wonder where he got the money. Maybe he inherited it. I heard that fishing is picking up, but Mac's thinking of switching from commercial fishing to sports fishing, a charter captain. At least that was the last I heard, his struggling with the idea. And, then here's his father's gambling. Studs will be out of a job. Oh well, none of my business.*

Maria opened the refrigerator and was surprised to find there were three bottles of wine. One was open, so she retrieved it and a glass on the counter, found a second glass in a cabinet. An hour. She might as well enjoy herself. *After all the word for the day is tranquility.*

Settling back in the seat next to Studs, she handed him his glass and was about to take a sip of her wine when Studs turned, tapped his glass to hers. "Here's to a beautiful day, Maria. And, to as many as you would like. I could give you that, you know."

"Umm. Sorry, Studs, but maybe, just maybe I've found the man who can give me what I'm looking for."

The NOAA radio in the galley crackled to life. A tropical depression was forming in the Gulf, heading east. The alert was drowned out with the noise of the Sun Rae's engine.

Chapter 49

Manny and Mac sat on two empty five-gallon paint cans facing each other. Sissy and Shrimp had left. Nothing more they could do today. The paint had to dry and then The Regina could be put back into the water ready to be sold ... or not.

Mac stared down at the yellowed envelope in his hand, the envelope that held the Arturo Perez bombshell—Patty Sue died of an overdose administered by Arturo and he had buried her on his family's land in Ocala.

"What are you going to do?" Manny asked, arms on his thighs, fingers picking paint off his thumb.

"You're the cop. What should I do?"

"Ex cop."

"Cop, Ex cop, you still think like a cop. We're talking about the woman my pops was going to marry, the woman for all these years, thirty-six, he believed had left him at the altar. I can't just walk up to him and say, 'guess what, Pops, You know that woman you thought left you at the altar? Well, she was killed.'" Mac looked up at Manny. "Sounds like Arturo should be convicted of murder, sent to the electric chair, except he's already dead."

"Involuntary manslaughter," Manny said looking down through his paint-spattered sneakers at the cement.

"What?"

"The letter. Says it was an overdose. He didn't plan to kill her. Strange that Maria saw him die ... but that was in New Orleans. Patty

Sue, at least from what's in this letter, is buried in Ocala, died on Anna Maria Island."

"Coincidence … Maria." Mac said.

"I don't believe in coincidences … not when crime is concerned. So, I asked you, what are you going to do?" Manny's eyes sought an answer from the man facing him.

"Can't talk to Pops. Not yet anyway. I'm not sure what he'd do. I'll talk to Maria first. Her mother was there that day."

"What about your mother … Regina?"

"I'll leave that up to Pops. From what he's told me I was conceived that day … the day he was left at the altar."

"Hard to figure how that happened."

"Yeah, seems like everyone close to me is tangled up in this … one way or another."

"Okay. I have to go. Promised Liz I'd be back for lunch. Call me after you talk to Maria. I'd like her take on the mystery person?"

"Mystery person?"

"Yeah, who led Arturo Perez to Patty Sue in the first place? Who called Arturo that day … the day of the wedding? Who told him that Patty Sue needed a fix? If what he said in the letter is true, why was he available? He certainly wasn't in New Orleans. I wonder if the ranch is still in the Perez family?"

Mac paced the dock clutching his cell phone. "Where is she?" he muttered.

He tried her cell again. The answering machine picked up. "Please leave a message with your name and number."

"Maria, where are you? Please call. You have the number."

Yeah, she has your number all right, he thought. He didn't want to call the hospital again, not after what happened the last time he tried to track her down ending in their big fight. He'd already left one message. *Maybe her mother. Oh yeah, stupid, she's sick. Even if Maria did call her she wouldn't remember if Maria told her where she was going. I don't even know the name of the home where's she's living. Well, there's one person who'll answer my call.*

"Manny, thank God someone answers their phone. I can't—"

"Nice timing, Mac. I was just going to call—"

"I can't find Maria. No answer on her cell, her home number, the hospital—"

"The hospital?"

"A nurse answered. She said Maria wasn't scheduled today. And now she's missing."

"When did you last talk to her?"

"It's been two days … what with the painting, taking the Calypso out for a run … trying to decide … Manny, where is she?"

"Tell you what, Stitch and I are just finishing lunch with the wedding planner at the Sandbar. We'll help you track her down. Where are you?"

"Same dock as this morning … where The Regina is up on the scaffolding."

Chapter 50

Mac continued pacing on the dock, cursing. Why wasn't Maria answering any of his messages? Looking up he saw Manny and Liz striding up the dock.

He closed his cell as Manny called out to him. "Any word from Maria?"

"Nothing—she still doesn't answer—home phone or her cell. Called the hospital again. Nothing. The nurse said it wasn't like her not to answer her cell. They tried to page her—no response. I guess there was a bus accident—church group. Emergency surgeries are backed up."

Liz stood beside Manny, her eyes darting from one man to the other. "Mac, I had a call from Crystal. I forgot to tell you in the excitement of meeting with the wedding planner."

"The crazy psychic?" Mac asked. "Now is not the time to—"

"I don't know about crazy, but she said she woke in the night. Felt she was drowning, but she didn't see herself. She saw Maria clear as day, her words 'clear as day.' Maria was on a boat arguing with a man."

"I don't suppose the wacko knew who the man was."

"Only that he was wearing a gold medal. She said it was the same medal in the picture Maria had shown to her when we met for the reading."

"Wasn't that Mac's picture?" Manny asked.

"Yes, but—"

"The man. Did Crystal see the man?" Manny asked skepticism written all over his face.

Liz shot him a wide-eyed look. "No, Sherlock. I asked her. She said he was fuzzy—only the medal."

Mac's hand felt the Saint Christopher medal under his white T-shirt. "That's not hard—Maria and I have been out on the boat several times and we've been fighting, and if it was my picture, well, Maria probably told her. The wacko's words are fuzzy—taking you for a ride, Liz."

"Wait, there's more. She said Maria had a gun in her hand. She said a storm was brewing."

"Maria doesn't own a gun," Mac said pulling his hair back out of his eyes, his breathing accelerating. What should he do?

Calypso was tethered to the dock. Her owner suggested Mac bring The Regina over where scaffolding was available. Mac had planned to take her out for a final run. *Hell, that was this morning.*

"Mac, Mac," Sissy shouted laughing, running up to Mac, Shrimp on his heels. "You'll never believe this. Studs left from another dock, Charlie's. You know those speedboats he rents, little cabin if they want to stay out overnight. He laughed when he saw us. Said that Studs sure knew how to pick 'em—boats and women. Charlie said Studs rented a Sun Rae, a very expensive beauty, and took off with a woman. But Charlie said she wasn't the usual kind of woman, if you know what I mean. Sophisticated. And, he paid—"

Mac, hands on hips, looked out over the water. Black clouds had begun to gather in the west turning the water from a light blue, to dark gray. "When did you last see Studs?"

"Last night at the bar," Shrimp said. "A blonde was making eyes at him and you know what that means. He took off with her. Of course, he usually shows up the next morning. I tried this morning but he didn't answer and didn't call back."

"Sissy, how would Charlie know if a woman was sophisticated?" Mac looked from one to the other. "Just so you two clowns know, I can't find Maria. I'm looking for her, not some blonde Studs picked up last night."

Manny looked at Mac. "If we don't have anything else to go on, why not head out ... let's see if we can find Maria, or Studs. Maybe crazy Crystal..."

Mac looked over at Calypso, called the owner that he was taking Calypso for run. Getting the okay, he shouted to Sissy and Shrimp to untie the lines as he jumped aboard signaling Manny and Liz to follow. "Let's go. I haven't heard from Maria. She's not a blonde, but maybe she's out with someone. It's the best lead we have. Hell, it's the only lead we have."

"Manny, you go," Liz said hanging back. "I'll wait here in case Maria shows up. If she does, I'll call your cell."

The lines untied, Sissy and Shrimp jumped onboard scampering to the stern grinning. They were always up for an adventure with their skipper.

Mac navigated Calypso away from the dock. Shaking his head, he pointed the bow of the boat into the gusty wind. "This is crazy, Manny. Do you know how big the Gulf is and we're out here going where? Because a fortune teller said some fuzzy man had Maria? It's like looking for a gold fish in the ocean."

Chapter 51

A gust of wind whipped over the dock. Liz, arms crossed over her chest, watched Calypso gain speed, the wake building in volume with each additional knot. She looked up at the gray sky. *Not too sinister, yet.* She'd heard of the Cortez Kitchen—a short walk. A cup of coffee might help to stimulate an idea, any idea to help find Maria would be better than nothing.

Turning to leave, buffeted from behind by the wind, Liz saw a woman. Her arms were wrapped tight around her body, head down as she shuffled against the stiff breeze. She seemed to be in distress, mumbling to herself.

Liz quickened her step.

Hurrying toward the woman Liz realized she knew her. It was Regina Macintyre. They had met once, dinner at the Sandbar with her son Mac.

"Regina, hi. You may not remember me, but Mac—"

Regina's head shot up, her eyes blank, face ashen, mumbling words so soft that Liz couldn't understand what she was trying to say. Regina's voice became stronger, the words strangling for freedom from her throat. She reached out grasping Liz's arm, her fingers digging into Liz's skin.

"I was told I could find Mac here. I must tell my son. Oh, Mac … my baby. What have I done? I …I… She can't have you. You're my

Mac. I have to stop her. Stop her for good. I'm sorry, Mac … so sorry. Maria won't be coming back."

"Regina, what are you saying?" Liz took hold of the woman's arms, searching her face for an answer.

Regina tried to speak but nothing came out … her mouth gaped open … knees buckled as her hands slid down clutching at Liz's arms, her hips … legs … crumpling to the ground.

"Help. Someone help," Liz yelled.

A man rushed up, knelt beside Regina, turned her onto her back as Liz called 9-1-1.

Hovering at the side of the bed Liz looked at the monitor—beeping, pausing, then beeping again. Regina's eyes were open, brows creased in pain, tubes leading from her body to the IV drip and the monitor overhead.

A nurse whispered to Liz that the woman's husband, Daniel Macintyre, had been notified that his wife had suffered a stroke and suggested he come quickly to the emergency entrance of the Manatee Memorial Hospital.

Liz nodded to the nurse and continued to stare down at Regina whose eyes stared back.

The doctor administered a shot into his patient's upper arm then glanced over at Liz shaking his head. Her friend was in a bad way.

Regina continued to stare at Liz, her fingers creeping across the sheet, inched up, touched Liz's hand, and with great effort tugged at Liz's fingers. "Purse … envelope …take."

Liz looked around—the chair, over at the bedside table. There on the shelf of the small table was the shoulder bag that was transported with Regina from the dock.

Grasping the bag, Liz pulled open the side pocket—a gas station receipt, earring, hanky—but no envelope. She unzipped the center compartment, her fingers frisking the inside, pushing a wallet, a checkbook, tube of lipstick, eyeliner pen, and an address book to the side revealing a white envelope. Nothing was written on the outside.

Liz held the envelope up to Regina.

Regina, her breathing labored, blinked twice.

Lifting the flap, Liz drew out a check—no payee, no date, the amount: $30,000, signed by Regina.

Regina groaned. Gasped. Her body shuddered. The monitor flatlined.

"Crash cart," the doctor ordered.

An intern pushed the cart to the anesthesiologist's side.

He yanked the paddles in the air.

"Clear."

Regina's body jerked. The monitor did not respond.

"Clear."

The monitor maintained the steady buzz … flat line.

"Clear."

There was no response from the lifeless woman.

Danny rushed into the room to see his wife lying on the bed. He was too late.

Regina was dead.

Chapter 52

The sky grew darker as the black clouds thickened. The wind remained steady. There were occasional gusts, but nothing alarming. Navigating Calypso, Mac shrugged his shoulders at Manny. The skipper had no idea where he was going. Sissy pressed the binoculars against his eyes scanning the horizon for a boat, for a woman, for Maria.

An hour passed.

"This is crazy, Manny. We're way out ... but no closer to finding her," Mac muttered.

"Keep going." Manny's cell rang. It was Liz. The connection was bad. Coupled with the noise of the motor, the only thing Manny heard was the name, Regina. He pointed to the cell, shook his head at Mac, and went to the cabin below, closing the door behind him.

"Okay, Stitch, repeat what you just said. All I got was Regina."

"Manny, she had a stroke on the dock. Right in front of me. I was scared stitchless ... sorry, I didn't mean that it was funny."

"Is she all right?"

"That's what I'm telling you—Regina's dead. The EMTs rushed her to the hospital but they couldn't save her. And, there's more—really weird."

"Stitch, I wouldn't call her dying weird—sad definitely but not—"

"No, no, listen. Before she, you know died, she asked for her purse, wanted me to look inside for an envelope. Manny, that woman had more stuff—"

"Stitch, what was in the envelope?"

"A check for thirty big ones."

"Thirty dollars?"

"Sherlock, I'm saying *biiiig* ones, like thirty-thousand dollars big."

"Who was the check made out to? Date?"

"Blank and blank but she signed it … I guess it was her signature. Wait a minute, I forgot to tell you what she said on the dock before the stroke. She said, let me read … I made a note at the hospital while the doctors worked on her. She said, quote … What have I done? She can't have you. You're my Mac. I have to stop her. Stop her for good. Maria won't be coming back ... end quote. What do you make of that?"

"I don't know …"

"Oh, and Danny ran into the room just as she died. I tell you, Sherlock, it was *creepy*."

"Meet me at the dock. I'll call you when we turn back, and, I'll let Mac know … about his mother. He can call the hospital, or his dad, if he wants to know more before we get back."

"Any sight of Maria?"

"No. Probably a wild goose chase. Catch you later."

Manny shoved his cell into his pants pocket and stepped out of the cabin. He didn't know how Mac was going to react to the news about his mother dying, so he sat next to him at the wheel for a few minutes, glancing at him several times out of the corner of his eyes, then reverting to the limitless water Calypso was grinding through.

"Okay, Manny what is it? Was that Liz?"

"Yeah. Your mother came down to the dock. I guess we had just left."

"I wonder why, unless she was looking for pops. Hang on. Big wave coming at us."

"Mac … your mother had a stroke."

Mac's head turned a little. His brow wrinkled, questioning.

"She died, Mac." Manny didn't get a chance to say anything else.

"Hey, Skipper," Sissy yelled. "There's a boat up ahead, looks like the one the guy at the boat rental described to Shrimp—a Sun Rae. My God, she's really going fast."

Mac stepped on the gas, sending Calypso flying over the water, full throttle, closing in on the boat Sissy spotted.

Chapter 53

The Sun Rae continued to knife through the water. The storm was building and there was no sign of Mac. Maria glanced at Studs, his jaw set, eyes peeled ahead. They were going fast over the building waves. She had to cling to the rail for support. Looking back all she saw was rough water. They were a long way from Cortez.

"Studs, looks like someone is trying to flag us down," Maria shouted.

His head snapped up. Studs recognized the structure. It was Calypso. There was no way he could lose her with Mac at the wheel, definitely not if he had seen Maria.

"Studs, you're a genius. You did it. You found Mac. Slow down," she said waving.

"The man was right, Manny. That's Studs and Maria's with him. What in the name of God is he doing with her?" Mac shouted closing the distance to the Sun Rae.

Shrimp laughed, "Maybe he put the make on her. Thought he could lure her away from you. That's a pretty fancy rig he's got there."

"Shut up you jug head," Sissy snapped. "He's seen us, Mac ... they're slowing down. Maria looks happy to see you. Can't say the same for Studs."

Mac pulled alongside the idling Sun Rae. "Sissy, tie up to Studs' boat," Mac said shifting his body over the side of Calypso, cursing as he fell into the Sun Rae, rubbing his arm and then his leg. "Well, you two, what's up, out for a picnic?" Mac snarled, getting to his feet as Manny and Sissy clumsily joined him on the Sun Rae. Shrimp, hands crossed over his chest stayed on Calypso. There was no way he was going to vault over the edge with his big frame.

"Mac, what are you talking about? We were trying to find you. Tell him, Studs." Maria moved away and sat on the edge of the boat opposite Mac. Her face clouding up, she was ready for a fight if that's what he wanted.

Everybody's head turned right hearing the roar of a boat racing in their direction, closing fast, so fast it was barely skimming the water.

"Studs, watch out," Manny yelled. "He's going to hit us."

A man, his platinum hair waving in the wind, swerved away at the last second. Its high rooster tail wake slammed against Calypso, swamping Studs' boat, water pouring over the side. Maria scrambled to get out of the way but she was too late. The force of the water washed her overboard. Mac jumped in after her, grasped her around the waist kicking hard to keep her head above water.

Studs grabbed the wheel. He had one last chance to take care of Maria for good. He turned the wheel hard to the left trapping Maria and Mac, pulling them into the motor, under the hull.

Sissy shoved Studs out of the way, yanked the wheel in the opposite direction and cut the engine. Manny dove in putting his arms around Maria as Mac went under again.

Shrimp yelled at Manny to grab the pole, the netting he was holding out from Calypso.

Manny lurched grasping the ring of netting, pulling Maria with him. Shrimp hung on to the pole with all his might pulling Manny with Maria alongside Calypso. Extending his hand to Maria, they locked fingers then wrists. Shrimp pulled her aboard as she gasped for air, coughing water out of her lungs.

With Maria out of the water, Shrimp turned to get Manny. At the same time, Sissy was waving his hand at Mac and cursing at Studs to stay back and not to do anything stupid.

Manny lunged back onto the Sun Rae and punched Studs in the nose. "You almost killed us, you bastard."

"Manny, give me hand, I can't hold Mac. He's slipping," Sissy yelled.

Together they managed to drag Mac over the edge of the Sun Rae.

"It was an accident," Studs screamed wiping blood from his nose. "You had no right to hit me."

"Accident? With your experience at sea?" Manny snapped.

Maria sat on a bench, leaning against the side of Calypso, trying to catch her breath, body shaking, terror in her eyes.

On the Sun Rae, Mac glowered at Studs. "Sissy, you and Shrimp take this creep back. Maria and Mac and I will take Calypso." Mac continued to look daggers at Studs. "I'll meet you at the Star Fish dock. You have some explaining to do, mister."

Chapter 54

The wind continued to gain strength buffeting the two boats heading to Cortez, one behind the other. Sissy, grim faced, was at the wheel of the Sun Rae. Shrimp sat on the bench behind him, glaring at Studs.

Studs sat on a bench, his back to Sissy, staring at the wake spewing on either side. His mind bounced from one excuse to another, sifting out what he was going to tell Mac. He was in the clear. As far as what Mac or the others knew, he had taken Maria out to find her fisherman. That's what she thought, so he was going to stick to that story.

Okay, he wouldn't collect thirty G's today in Key West. Whenever his benefactor called, asking what happened, well, he'd say the timing wasn't right, but he'd promise to fulfill his end of the bargain. As far as Mac was concerned, Studs didn't owe him anything. When, or if, he sold The Regina, he was out of a job. Mac had made that perfectly clear.

The thing that bothered Studs was the platinum-haired guy who almost crashed into them. He'd never seen him before—so white—hair and skin. *A ghost? No, more like the devil. Sure scared me. Maria looked terrified too. He was leering at me. I'm not going to wait at the dock. I don't care what Mac says. I'll go to my room. Settle down. Tomorrow ... tomorrow I'll talk to Mac. Tell him he has it all wrong. How dare he think I was making a pass at his precious doctor. Besides, that's what Maria is going to say ... same thing. Mac may even be sorry he accused me of such a thing ... hire me back instead of Shrimp.*

The boat lurched forward, picked up speed. Sissy wanted to get back to Cortez before the storm hit.

Calypso cruised toward Cortez piercing each wave with her bow. Sissy was back about a fifty yards in the Sun Rae but getting closer. The clouds continued to build in the west and an occasional shower splattered the window. Mac was at the wheel in the shelter of the cabin. Maria and Manny sat on canvas chairs behind Mac talking about the wedding plans—anything but what had happened within the last hour. Manny did most of the talking. Maria stared, transfixed, looking through him, uttering an occasional, "Oh."

All had blankets draped over their shoulders that Mac found in one of the cabinets.

"Manny, can you take the wheel? I want to talk to Maria before we dock."

"Sure." Manny flashed a tentative smile at Maria as he and Mac traded seats.

Mac looked at Maria, sighed, pulled the blanket across his chest feeling a chill under his wet clothes. "Manny had a call from Liz just before we saw you and Studs."

Maria didn't say anything only looking back at Mac, pulling her blanket tighter around her body.

"Liz ran into my mother on the dock. Long and short ... my mother had a stroke. Liz called for help. Regina died at the hospital."

Maria didn't move continuing to stare at Mac. "Did she have a weak heart?" she asked in hushed tone.

"Not that I know of."

Manny glanced around, "Mac, Liz also said there was a check in Regina's purse—no payee, but she signed it—for thirty thousand dollars. Any idea what that was for?"

"Haven't a clue. She never talked about money, her money."

"Maybe she was going to help you buy this boat. Calypso. Seems like she's sound ... handles well. We certainly put her through her paces this afternoon," Manny said with a hint of a chuckle.

Mac saw Maria stiffen.

"I never talked to my mother about Calypso—only generalities about switching from commercial fishing ... maybe we should check with your crazy psychic."

"Seems like your mother was a possessive woman," Manny said glancing around at the couple.

"She was, but why would you say that?" Mac asked leaning forward elbows on his knees, hands under his chin.

"Liz said she was rambling on just before she died about no one was going to have her Mac."

"Maybe she was thinking of pops. She always kept watch over him unless he snuck out to the casino."

"Hey, here comes Sissy. Guess he's anxious to get back," Manny said acknowledging Sissy's wave.

Mac looked out the window. "Sissy's a worrywart. Probably wants to beat the storm," he said turning back to Maria. "So, what was going on with you and Studs today?"

"I told you. He was taking me to find *you,* but you jumped all over him ... and ... why would you ever think I was having a picnic with him?" Maria clutched her blanket tighter.

"I was worried about you, Maria. And, yes, I admit I was a bit jealous once—"

"A bit? You've practically been stalking me—call my house, my cell, and the hospital ... please, tell me you didn't call the hospital today?"

Mac's head hit the back of the chair, eyes up at the ceiling as he crossed his arms over his head. "Yeah, I did."

Maria leaned back. Her hand began to tremble. "Mac, how could you? I—"

"Listen, Maria, I was worried and so was the hospital. They were also trying to reach you. But, I guess you were too busy to answer their call."

"For your information, I forgot my phone."

"And your pager in your rush to meet with Studs?"

"Yes, my pager—for God's sake, Mac, get off the big brother act!"

"Please, don't be mad. I won't do it again, and you're safe now. What happened today is over."

"Yes, it's over ... all over."

Chapter 55

The NOAA radio sputtered to life warning that the storm moving east over the Gulf to the west coast of Florida was now a tropical depression at thirty-eight-mile-per-hour sustained winds. It was expected to be upgraded shortly to a tropical storm, with increased wind speed close to seventy-three miles-per-hour.

Mac switched the radio off preparing to dock, careful not to cut the engine too soon so he could make adjustments preventing Calypso from banging hard against the pilings.

"Mac, how about you and Maria joining Liz and me for a bite to eat. She called and suggested it … wants to know how we can help with you and your dad."

"Tell Liz thanks, Manny, but I want to go straight home," Maria replied. "I need a hot shower and check in with the hospital. *Explain my delinquency*," she finished with a sharp look at Mac.

Mac wasn't backing down.

He hadn't done anything wrong.

"Is your car here?" he asked locking up Calypso as Manny helped Maria out of the boat.

"It's up the road—the boat rental."

"Okay, I'll drive you." Mac said jumping onto the dock, glancing around for Studs.

"I can make it. Thanks anyway. Here comes Liz. I'll say goodbye to her and be on my way. Thanks, Manny … for everything."

"No problem ... happy none of us drowned," he chuckled giving Maria a quick hug.

Maria took a step away, hesitated, took another and then whirled around facing Mac. Her face tortured, she stepped back to him, grasped his face searing her lips into his. His arms enveloped her, held tight. She broke from his arms and quickly walked up the dock.

"What was that all about?" Manny asked.

"I don't know. Did you see the look on her face?"

"Yeah."

The uneasy feeling he had when he and Maria argued on the boat grew stronger, seeping through his body, as he watched her stop to talk to Liz. They hugged and then Liz jogged up to Manny. They embraced as he whispered in her ear, "I love you and I'll tell you everything later."

Liz smiled at Manny—message received. She turned and hugged Mac. "I'm so sorry about your mother. It happened fast. She didn't suffer if that's any consolation."

Mac nodded his head. Said nothing. He didn't want to talk.

"Where's Studs?" Manny asked. I thought you told him to meet you here."

"Looks like a no show. Sissy called just before we docked. He'd been in almost an hour with that rocket, the Sun Rae Studs rented. He and Shrimp had had enough for one day. The three of them went their separate ways."

"Well, Maria wasn't hungry. How about you guys? We can run up to the Cortez Kitchen." Liz pulled the hood of her yellow slicker over her head. The rain had started and they ran for cover in the Star Fish Market.

The screen door banged shut with a gust of wind just as Mac's cell rang. His face turned grim. He stepped to the case of fish lying on crushed ice, his back to Manny and Liz. He was listening intently to whoever was on the other end.

Manny and Liz exchanged glances then back to Mac as he turned back to them. Rubbing his face, he looked out the screen door at the rain beginning to pool on the gravel road.

"Studs is dead. Shot less than an hour ago in the room he rented down the street. He and another guy, a Wallace Gutfeld. Gutfeld had an ID tag, Tulane Hospital, New Orleans. Both shot. A gun was found in the hand of the Wallace fellow. Maybe he shot Studs and then himself. That was my cop friend on the phone. That's all he knows. He's waiting for ballistics to learn more."

"Who called 9-1-1?" Manny and Liz asked in unison.

"He didn't know. Someone heard the shot. Called 9-1-1. Everyone knows everyone in this town. Even though Maria's not going to want to hear from me, I think I'd better let her know. Better from me than the television."

Mac, his cell still in his hand, tapped Maria's code.

The conversation was brief.

He shut the phone. Stared at the dead fish lying on the ice.

"What did she say," Liz asked.

"Thanks for calling and hung up."

Chapter 56

Upgraded to a tropical storm, packing winds at sixty-seven miles per hour, the black clouds turned early evening to night, bending trees to the breaking point. Heavy rain turned roads into streams.

Maria pulled into her garage, pushed the button sliding the garage door to the floor—a barrier to the raging storm outside. Sitting in the car, her body trembling, she rested her head on the cool leather of the steering wheel.

"What am I going to do?" she whispered.

The vision of Crystal staring at her, warning of danger, filled her mind.

Fumbling with the door handle, she stepped out of the car. The overhead garage light flickered but remained on following a sharp crack of lightning.

Testing that the garage door was shut tight, she hurried up the stairs to the main floor. Flipping on the small table light at the top of the stairs, she looked sharply left and right—so many doors to check. She quickly stepped to each—front door, French doors, slider to the dining oasis which seemed sinister—bushes and trees clawing at the screens. Realizing she only checked the garage door, she raced down the stairs to check that all the doors on the ground floor were secure—the slider to the pool, the back door leading to the garden and the path to the beach, the door to the smaller garage filled with bicycles for the owner's and guest's enjoyment to explore the island.

Satisfied that all doors were locked, Maria ran back up the stairs to the main floor.

With a sigh, a second look around, she walked down the hall to her bedroom. *Get out of these damp clothes ... then a hot shower ... I'll feel better. That's what I'll do.*

Refreshed in a dry pair of tan capris and a white silk blouse, it was time for a cup of hot coffee. She had to think, think about all the ramifications of her decision. A bolt of lightning illuminated the room quickly returning the space to the dim light of the table lamp.

What am I going to do?

For two years I felt safe, watched the news, read the headlines in newspapers ... but Bennett and then Donovan arrived. They had put the puzzle together with me in the center, the missing piece. A star, no, a critical witness they said who could start the process to bring the drug lords down—not through tax evasion, oh no, for murder.

Padding to the kitchen, the cool wood of the floor under her bare feet, Maria setup the single-shot coffeemaker with her favorite blend. The musical sound of water gurgling as it seeped through the container of ground beans was soothing, the aroma familiar. Her nerves let go a little, just a little, as she lifted the mug breathing in the steam rising from the dark liquid.

She curled up on the swing, clutched a pillow to her lap and took a sip, letting the hot coffee ease over her tongue, caress her throat, warm her body.

Suddenly a bolt of lightning filled the sky. Maria held her breath waiting for the explosion of thunder. The crack was instant, close. Along with the lightning came the realization that she was not safe, but could she really do it?

Quickly returning to the kitchen, she put her coffee cup in the sink, reached for the bottle of red wine, a goblet. Filling the glass she swallowed several gulps hoping to ease her nerves. She forced herself to breathe deeply ... breathe ... breathe ... breathe.

Walking to the French doors she looked out at the railing bordering the narrow deck, out over the silhouette of trees, out to the beach, the roar of the pounding surf penetrating the closed doors.

A drop of wine spilled over the edge of the goblet as her body trembled again. She hadn't revealed, didn't tell Donovan everything she saw that day. She'd held back hoping she wouldn't be pulled into their investigation. Hadn't told him she would never forget the man in the white coat over striped pants, never forget his face—no pigmentation only white white skin, white hair, and his eyes, pink eyes, blood in the capillaries of the iris. She had expunged his image from her mind until today, the boat careening toward her. It was him. He'd found her.

A bolt of lightning, bigger than the last, turned night to day and there he was, walking up the path from the beach. The Albino.

The table lamp went out. Electricity cut.

Trembling, Marie traced her lips with her fingers, felt the heat of Mac's lips on hers. Felt the strength of his arms around her. He was in danger because of her.

Maria fumbled for her cell, tapped the code, lifted the tiny lifeline to her ear. The call was answered before the first ring ended.

"Donovan here."

"I'm ready. I'll do it. The Albino … he's here."

"We know. Thank God you called. Don't go outside, Dr. Grayson. I'm only a few houses away—we've been watching. I repeat, do not go outside. Wait! Don't open the door until you hear my voice—code word: chapel. Three minutes. Don't call anyone. Your life is at stake. Three minutes."

Maria didn't close her cell. One call. She had to make one call.

"Hello, Sunrise House."

"This is Dr. Grayson. I have to speak to my mother."

"I'm so sorry, Dr. Grayson. She's been very agitated today for some reason. We gave her a sedative to calm her down. She's asleep."

"Please, I must talk to her. Check. Maybe she's awake."

… a bolt of lightning, crack of thunder, darkness.

"Hello."

"Mother, it's me, Maria."

"Who?"

"Your daughter, Maria. Mother, I'm in trouble. Remember Arturo Perez?"

"My friend Artie? Dear Artie. I need him. Please tell him, whoever you are, to come to me. Hurry. Dear Artie, always there when I need him."

"I love you, Mother."

Chapter 57

It was five o'clock. Almost twenty-four hours since Mac had seen Maria, seen her walking up the dock, walking away from him. The storm had crossed the Florida peninsula and was blowing itself out over the Atlantic.

Twenty-four hours.

Mac paced in his trailer. Grabbed his coffee mug and went outside. Walked around the bushes then sat on the top step of his trailer, the late afternoon sun hitting him in the eyes. A crow squawked overhead. The humidity left in the wake of the storm was stifling—the underarms of his T-shirt damp as was the back of his shirt. "I don't care what she says. I've waited long enough. I'm calling," he muttered wiping a fresh bead of sweat from his brow with a stroke of his arm.

I'll be cool, ask if there was any damage to the house. It won't matter if I call her on her home phone ... her cell ... or the hospital.

Throwing the balance of his coffee on an Aloe plant sending a gecko skittering for cover, Mac retrieved his cell from his shorts pocket and selected the code for the beach house.

He counted the rings—four. No answer. No voice asking him to leave a message.

He selected the code for her cell. Same thing. No answer. No request to leave a message.

His finger hovered over the hospital code. She'd been adamant that he not track her down at the hospital.

"So, she gets upset. Too bad. I have to know she's all right."

He punched the hospital number.

"Manatee Memorial Hospital, Emergency."

"Hi. Is Dr. Grayson there?"

"No, Sir. Dr. Grayson is no longer at this hospital."

"What? Where did she go?"

"That's all I know, Sir."

Mac stared at the phone.

Impossible!

Jamming the cell into his pocket, he charged down the path to his truck. It was time to have it out with the good doctor. *No more of her cat and mouse games. She must be home ... not answering my calls.*

Driving over the bridge from Cortez onto Anna Maria Island, he tried her home phone again. Four rings. No Answer. Still no request to leave a message.

He pulled into the driveway. Jogged up the stairs to the front door and pushed the doorbell.

"Come on, Maria. Let's talk," he called out.

He knocked hard on the door.

The door swung open.

"Maria ... it's Mac."

There was no reply.

Mac pulled out his cell.

"Manny, I'm at Maria's house. She didn't answer any of my calls. Just now the front door swung open when I knocked."

"She's not there?" Manny asked.

"No. Can you come over? It's just down the street from your motel—Liz knows. Something's wrong. I think I'd better not go in alone."

"You're right. Stay outside. Liz and I will be right over. We're just finished grabbing a bite down the street at Ginny's & Jane E's."

Manny and Liz ran up the steps to Mac standing at the top of the stairs.

"Still no word from Maria?" Manny asked.

"No. I left the door open. Just as I found it."

"Okay, let's go in," Manny said.

He and Liz followed Mac into the living room.

"There's a coffee cup in the sink … some coffee still in it," Mac said glancing around the kitchen.

"Wine glass on the dining room table," Liz said. "Can't be more than a few sips gone."

Mac walked down the hall. "Nothing out of place in the bedroom," he called out. Returning to the living room, he looked out the French doors, turned and looked at the swing.

"It's eerie," Liz said. "It's like she's here but she isn't."

"I'll take a look upstairs," Mac said.

"Do these stairs lead to the garage?" Manny asked.

"Yeah. Go down, have a look. See if her car is there."

Liz hurried down the steps with Manny. He opened the door to the garage and Liz peeled off to the left to check the pool area. They met back at the bottom of the stairs, both nodding that they'd found nothing.

Returning to the front door the three stood, taking a few steps one way then another, hands on hips.

"Nothing out of the ordinary," Liz said.

"The car is gone," Manny said looking over at Mac.

An empty feeling enveloped Mac—evidence Maria had been here but a feeling that she never was. His cell rang piercing the quiet of the empty house.

Yanking the cell from his pocket, Mac pressed it to his ear listening to someone on the other end. "Thanks ... thanks for letting me know," he said slumping onto the swing. His hand dropped to his thigh, his fingers slack, the cell easing from his open palm to the swing cushion.

Manny knew the look. How many times had he given bad news to a loved one? He squatted in front of Mac and saw tears forming in his eyes.

Liz, standing beside Manny her hand on his shoulder, also recognized the look on Mac's tortured face.

"What happened, Mac? Who was that?" Manny asked, his voice soft, waiting for the words.

"My cop friend. Maria's car was found about one o'clock this morning. Interstate 75 near Ocala. The car had rolled … going too fast for the curve. The gas tank exploded. Only charred metal left. Whoever was driving was incinerated."

Epilogue

Five Months later — Anna Maria Island

The January sun warmed the motel room sending slices of rainbow light across the carpet. Liz opened her eyes a crack. Manny was curved around her body snoring softly into her mop of red curls. They had been married four months and she loved him more than she did on their wedding day.

They had returned to Anna Maria Island accepting Mac's gift. He had invited them to meet him at the Cortez dock for a day of fishing out in Gulf. His way of saying thank you for their help last summer.

"Hey, Mr. Salinas," Liz whispered.

Manny felt a light nudge from an elbow in his stomach.

"Umm. What, Mrs. Salinas."

"Love it … Mrs. Salinas. Has a nice ring to it, don't you think? Of course, professionally it's still Stitchway."

"Go back to sleep, Mrs. Salinas."

"Can't." Liz rolled over. Tickled his moustache. "Mac said to be at the dock eight sharp."

Manny pulled her close, her head tucked under his chin. "Do we have time to fool around, Mrs. Salinas?"

"Umm. Always, Mr. Salinas."

Cortez

Liz and Manny strolled down the dock—perpetual smiles on their faces, each carrying two cups of coffee.

"Would you look at that, Manny?" Liz said. "Mac renamed Calypso to Patty Sue."

"Hey, you two," Mac called out standing on the aft deck of his boat. "Pops and I were just saying we hoped you'd bring coffee with you. Hop on. Welcome aboard the Patty Sue." Mac lifted the extra cup of coffee from Liz's hand and helped her on board. Manny was right behind her and handed his extra cup to Danny who stepped out of the cabin.

"Beautiful day for fishing, son," Danny said folding back the flap on the lid of the coffee cup, and taking along sip. "Thanks for the coffee, Manny."

"That it is, Pops. What you say we get this party underway?"

"Right-O, Captain. Fire her up. Manny and I will tend to the lines. Elizabeth, why don't you have a seat on that deck chair I set out for you?"

"I don't have a fishing license," Liz said sitting in her designated chair and zipping up her red windbreaker against the January air.

"All part of Macintyre and Son, Sports Fishing Charter, little lady—license, rod, and bait. It's up to you to catch the fish," Danny said with a grin on his face. This is what he called living.

Mac climbed to the flying bridge and soon the Patty Sue was cutting through the Gulf waters, throwing a sparkling wake in the rays of the sun.

Manny followed and sat next to Mac. The men smiled at each other but at this moment were content to share the beautiful morning, the cool breeze, and the blue water, keeping thoughts of the last time they were together to themselves. Manny glanced sideways a few times to see how his friend was coping with the loss of Maria. Mac remained intent on the expanse of water ahead—wasn't joking, wasn't laughing, with a touch of sadness around his eyes.

"I miss her, Manny," Mac said staring ahead. He didn't move. He could have been talking to a fly on the window.

This was always the hard part of Mac's day—the hum of the engine enveloping him in a sadness of what might have been, but now will never be. Patty Sue breached every wave, the bow rising then crashing down, like his life. Hope and promise one day only to be dashed the next.

"Did they find any DNA … at the crash site?" Manny asked taking a sip of coffee.

"Nope. Fire so hot it burned everything. Only twisted metal—some of that melted."

"Your dad seems to be doing well. Drinking? Gambling?"

"Ever since Mom died he seems to be a new man. I think she kept him on such a tight rein it strangled him. But, when he bunks with me in the trailer, he roams around. Talks a lot in his sleep. Says he's talking to Patty Sue. Swears she comes to see him. Maria asked him once to come with me to dinner at the beach house she was tending."

"Did he?"

"I described where the house was located, just off of Gulf Drive. He said he knew the house. He'd been there a few times when Mrs. Parsons and Patty Sue were making plans for the wedding. No, he didn't want to go into that house … ironic, huh? Pops and I both lost a woman from that house."

The two men sipped their coffee looking out at the beauty of the sea, leaving words unsaid mixing beauty with horror.

On the aft deck Danny sat next to Liz, instructing her on how to bait her rod, how to caste, and how to reel in the fish. Satisfied her lesson was over, for the time being anyway, she laid the rod down on the deck and leaned back in the chair loving the warmth of the sun on her face. Squinting at Danny, she said, "I see Mac changed the name to Patty Sue."

"Yup. Named her after the love of my life. That was before, Regina, you understand."

"I understand."

"He was able to trade in The Regina for Calypso. Paid off the balance with some of the money his mother left him in her will. Did you notice what he painted on the side?"

"No. What?"

"Macintyre and Son, Sports Fishing Charter. Both sides. Nice?"

"Very nice."

"Suppose you know all about Patty Sue, how we learned what happened to her. The letter."

"Yes, I do, Mr. Macintyre."

"Danny. Please, call me Danny. Well, the week after Maria ... just can't say she burned up. Anyway, Mac and I went to look for Patty Sue's remains following the description in the letter that Arturo Perez sent to me. Foolishness that I hadn't open it ... but, I wasn't doing much reading at that time," Danny said with a chuckle.

"What happened? Did the Perez people let you on the land?" Liz asked.

"Well, it was a funny thing. The caretaker, Roberto something, came to the gate. Mac told him what we wanted, shows him the letter, and the man let us in. There was a For Sale sign just outside the gate. Mac asked him about it."

"What did he say?" Liz shielded her eyes from the sun sitting up straight, leaning forward in her chair to hear what Danny was saying over the noise of Patty Sue's motor.

"He said that the Perez family members, those who lived on the horse farm, left one night without saying a word. Still hasn't heard from them. Like ... they up and abandoned the farm. Shortly after that, some IRS agent came by with a realtor. He said the property had been repossessed, up for sale, non-payment of taxes. The realtor hammered in the sign, with the help of the agent, and they both asked the caretaker to stay on until the property was sold. The agent told Roberto that he would be paid to watch over the place until someone bought it. After that ... well, that would be up to the new owners."

"Wow. And did you find Patty Sue?"

"Yup. Course, the land had changed—trees grew, brush was overgrown, but we did. The caretaker had a backhoe. Grave wasn't deep but deep enough she wasn't disturbed ... we found her."

A brisk breeze circled over the deck. "Feel that, Elizabeth?"

Liz nodded rolling the sleeves down on her windbreaker. "Turning chilly."

"Naw. That's Patty Sue. I know. I've seen her. Said she was going to watch over me. She sure has done that." Danny chuckled staring out at the wake behind the boat.

"Where is Patty Sue buried now?"

"Mac and I found a nice spot ... on my dad's land ... well, the land he left to Mac ... where his trailer is. Nice headstone ... small ... but pretty ... just like my Patty Sue."

Now too warm, Liz unzipped the windbreaker, frowning at Danny behind his back. *Could there be any truth to what he said. Was Patty Sue here?*

"This should be a good spot," Mac called out cutting the engine. "Grouper and amberjacks usually run around here. Hey, Pops. Let's drop anchor. Give these two a chance to try their luck."

The next two hours were hectic—baiting fish, reeling in the line checking that the bait was still there or if a clever fish had taken the treat avoiding the hook. Danny took Liz under his wing. He was rewarded for his efforts when together they fought with a big grouper, finally landing him. Danny estimated it was at least twenty pounds.

Then Manny reeled in two amberjacks in a row. "Who's winning the fishing derby now, Mrs. Salinas?"

"Hah! I'm not done—"

She was cut short by a tug on her line. Laughing crazy, she reeled up a red snapper tying her husband's tally.

"Believe that's a ten pounder, Elizabeth," Danny said removing the hook and tossing the fish on top of the ice in the chest.

"You guys keep fishing if you want, but I'm starved," Mac said. "Pops picked up sandwiches, sides of cheesy grits and hush puppies if anyone's interested." He laughed as the fishing poles were immediately stashed in their holders. Danny pulled out more canvas chairs, and they dug into the basket of food.

"Ever see that creep again who almost ran us over that day?" Manny asked popping a hush puppy in his mouth.

"Nope, never did," Mac said. "Pops and I did take a run over to New Orleans for a couple of days. We paid our respects to the Parsons. They buried Regina in the family plot."

"How did that go? Were they polite?" Liz asked.

"Polite enough, wouldn't you say, son? We only stayed a few minutes. Probably because they didn't ask us to come inside." Danny laughed slapping his thigh.

"We stopped at Sunrise House ... the people who are taking care of Maria's mother." Mac looked at Liz's raised brows. "I know, I know, but I just had to ask if Maria had been in touch. Praying that someone ... saw her. The woman in charge, looked at me strangely, then said that Dr. Grayson hadn't come in or called, and that Marianne spent her days mumbling the name Artie."

"So, another strong contact to Arturo Perez—Maria saying she didn't see him die, the letter Perez sent to you, Danny, and then Mrs. Grayson fixated on his name. Go figure. I'll take another one of those beers. Anyone else?" Manny asked.

Everyone nodded in the negative.

"When we were in New Orleans I also looked up that lawyer guy, Bennett. There's a cool character. He said his part of the Perez case was closed. Said he had no idea what that agent, Donovan was up to. I felt he knew more, but I didn't press it," Mac said. "I've asked my cop friend several times if he found out who killed Studs and that other guy. He just keeps telling me that it's under investigation. Something about jurisdiction—the other guy was from out of state."

"Mac, tell Manny and Liz about Studs and your mother."

"Oh, yeah, that's another mystery. When pops and I went through her papers, settled up her estate, we found a cancelled check—made out to cash—$5000. Wasn't endorsed. But, when I was questioned about Studs' murder, the investigator asked if I had any idea where Studs got the money that was deposited in his account and withdrawn the day before he died. The amount was $5000. Coincidence?" Mac asked looking at Manny.

"Well, you know how I feel about coincidences—not." Manny said taking a swig of beer.

"Son, if your mother hired Studs to take Maria away from you, then I guess we could take a leap and say she tried to keep Patty Sue from me."

"That *is* a leap, Pops."

"Well, there's still the mystery person?" Manny said. "If Perez is to be believed, he was contacted by someone to see Patty Sue, give her drugs. Danny, as you recall it, weren't there three people with Patty Sue the day she disappeared: Mrs. Parsons, Regina, and Marianne Grayson. Mr. and Mrs. Parsons didn't want you to marry Patty Sue but it's unlikely that they would have had their daughter killed or ever led her into drugs. That leaves Regina and Marianne."

"Good old Artie," Liz said. "Gave us everything but who called him."

Manny and Liz stashed the trash from their lunch into the basket, then sat back enjoying the view of the water and a cargo ship off in the distance making its way to port.

Mac lit up his once-a-day cigar holding out the small pack to Manny, then Liz. Liz smiled at his thoughtfulness but both declined. "Guess we should head back," Mac said taking a puff. "How do you want to handle the fish when we dock? Give them to the fish house to clean?"

Danny looked up grinning. "We'll clean them. Cut into fillets—all part of the—"

"I know, I know—Macintyre and Son, Sports Fishing Charter. I vote we clean ... no ... you clean the fish," Liz said smiling at Danny.

"Okay," Mac said laughing at Liz. "And, we can go even further ... not part of our service but in your case we will make an exception. When are you two heading back to Port Orange?"

"Tomorrow. Staying tonight."

"What do you think, Pops? We could freeze the fillets over night. Mr. and Mrs. Salinas can pick them up in the morning on their way home."

"Works for me ... but only for Mr. and Mrs. Salinas," Danny said smiling at Liz.

"Oh, wait, one more piece of news. Pops asked if I could introduce him to Crystal. He wanted to tell her about Patty Sue. This was before we went to New Orleans—months ago."

"And, did you meet Madame Crystal, Danny?" Liz asked.

"No. It goes under unfinished business. She was in the hospital. Her doctor said she was suffering from exhaustion. Seems all her spirits were colliding. The doctor had traced her illness back to a session a few days before Maria disappeared."

Turning serious, Mac, with Manny following, climbed back up to the flying bridge and turned the Patty Sue back to Cortez. The men smiled at each other but at this moment were again content to share the beautiful morning in silence. Manny glanced sideways a few times. Mac remained intent on the expanse of water ahead—wasn't joking, wasn't laughing, tears filling his eyes.

"Did you learn anything of interest today, Miss Stitchway?"

"That I did, Sherlock. Play your cards right and I may even share them with you tonight."

Manny turned her into his arms with a very warm embrace, then hand-in-hand they continued to stroll up the dock.

"Manny, do you think there's a possibility that Maria accepted that FBI Agent's offer … you know, the whole new identity thing to protect his witness?"

"Well's there's her car … exploding as it rolled. The police say she died in the fiery crash. I do know that finding her car ended Mac's search."

"Umm. I'd like to think she's out there somewhere."

The End

Books by Mary Jane Forbes

FICTION

Murder by Design, Series:
Murder by Design – Book 1
Labeled in Seattle – Book 2
Choices, And the Courage to Risk – Book 3

Novel
The Baby Quilt ... *a mystery!*
The Message...Call me!

Elizabeth Stitchway, Private Investigator, Series:
The Mailbox – Book 1
Black Magic, An Arabian Stallion – Book 2
The Painter – Book 3
Twister – Book 4
The Fisherman – Book 5

House of Beads Mystery Series:
Murder in the House of Beads – Book 1
Intercept – Book 2
Checkmate – Book 3
Identity Theft – Book 4

Short Stories
Once Upon a Christmas Eve, a Romantic Fairy Tale
The Christmas Angel and the Magic Holiday Tree

NONFICTION
Authors, Self Publish With Style

Visit: www.MaryJaneForbes.com

CPSIA information can be obtained at www.ICGtesting.com
Printed in the USA
LVOW12s0232290713

345008LV00002BA/74/P